Donna
OR
THE SPHERE

Copyright © 2023 by Donnalu Evans

What if?

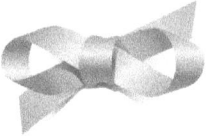

Prologue

Screaming for his tormentor's release, Randy begged to end the brutalization. The bright lights above blinded him as fear overwhelmed his young mind causing him to blackout.

The cloaked forms use sharp metal objects to extract parts of his organs for their experiments, never acknowledging the anguish they cause the young man or his friend, lying unconscious, on the table beside him.

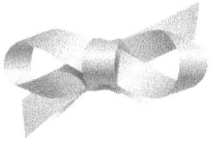

Dedication

To my husband, Mike, who believes in me.

DONNALU EVANS

ORIGIN THE SPHERE

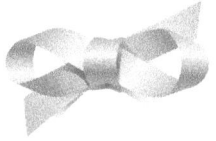

Chapter One

A mysterious glowing object skyrocketed into the earth's atmosphere appearing only seconds in the night sky, screaming as it maneuvered toward its destination. The impact vibrates the land mass causing the earth to burst open as the article embedded itself into the mountainside. In the moonlight above the crater, little was observed to acknowledge what transpired and that the collision would change life, as we humans know it, forever.

• • ⸙ • •

"SEVEN, SIX, ONE, SIX, Airy, repeat these numbers, you must.... Buzz, Buzz." The clock hummed a third time waking Airy alleviating her of an annoying dream. This was the fourth time she remembered dreaming about numbers and every time she'd awaken with a splitting headache. Glancing at the clock on the table she realized the time was late and needed to hurry to the university she didn't want to miss the two-hour lecture given by her former professor on, 'Theory of Evolution and Change. Did Man Exist Before?'

Walking quickly across the lawn a freebee zoomed through the air right for her. She screamed, "Watch it!" In dodging the object, the hot coffee she carried in her left hand splashed out of its container scalding her skin. Today started with her exasperating nightmare, then oversleeping, and now these infuriating kids, outside her apartment building, and their damn toy, she wondered what more dissatisfy awaited her. Hurrying, into her car she wiped off the liquid blowing on her still-burning wrist.

The audience's attention was superglue on the professor as he stressed how the world changed significantly every couple of thousand years or more. How land and environment as well as inhabitants are always evolving. He went so far as to say, that we as people could have lived before, and to this date, because of the lack of scientific proof, it is just a theory. That the earth could be older than thought and that man didn't develop as slowly as documented. All our evidence to date could be wrong. Markers set forth to test carbon dating and radiometric dating could be off by thousands or millions of years and purely invalid. Deeply fascinated by the subject, Airy twirled a pen between her fingers as the lecture continued.

This was Professor Morard's first lecture to the university on a theory he proposed. Next semester he planned a new class called, 'Theories and Answers,' for anyone interested in taking the idea to the next level.

As Airy listened, she considered the possibilities, she knew it was irresponsible to think with new finds in the last ten years, which were not logical to what we know, that mankind could have made mistakes in calculating the time periods of artifacts or even when life began.

"The continent was still called Pangaea, one supercontinent when life began. By the end of the dinosaur era, it had already broken apart into the seven continents we have now," the professor took a breath and then continued. "Man is thought to have developed only two million years ago. If we are to believe human life began after dinosaurs were extinct, why are there paintings by cavemen of the dinosaurs including ones with feathers that we didn't discover until recently?"

Airy thoughts were swarming and the pen between her fingers took flight and hit the young woman beside her.

Dee looked up from her notes and glared questioning at her friend.

Airy whispered, "Sorry."

The professor cleared his throat in front of them, "Ladies, will you answer the question for everyone to hear? What patterns do you see emerging in evolution?"

Dee glared at her friend. Airy knew that look and rose from her seat to respond to the professor's inquiry, "There is a significant pattern of approximately 2.5 to 4 thousand years for every evolution to begin, and it seems as though the period is approaching. However, human interaction with the environment has hastened that time scale, so we could begin it as early as today."

"And can anyone tell me which human-like species came first and the period?"

A man in the seat behind and to the right of Airy raised his hand and stood to answer. His height was barely five feet and he looked considerably older than most of the students, somewhere in his thirties, Airy thought to herself.

"Homo habilis are said to be the first true human species coming from East and Southern Africa about two million years ago, but scientists debate this saying they were still part of the austral piths, though more advanced. Homo habilis made stone tools and austral piths are more like an ape; however, in recent years that concept has changed to make them closely related, with both species creating stone tools. Approximately 30,000 BCE started the Old Stone Age nearly 2.6 million years ago. Lucy, a female hominin from Ethiopia was discovered in 1974 and dated to 3.2 million years ago, older than the Stone Age. An article I read in 2018, said carbon dating and our whole history of human evolution needs to be pushed back several hundred thousand years. So, is science saying carbon dating is wrong, and therefore all theories before and forward are erroneous? Is there a new method of dating?" the man asked.

"No, and it's not as simple as that, but you are proving my position with the facts you quoted," the professor stated, "Some hominines thought to bury their dead and this proves that they were more sophisticated than previously believed. What I am proposing is that man, like you and I, not a caveman, in simple terms could have existed millions of millions of years ago. In the early part of the 20th century, scientists were still uncertain about how old the earth was, they thought it to be millions of years old versus the 4.5 billion years that is believed today. The layers of rock make it hard to determine. Today radiometric dating which focuses on the decay of atoms from one chemical element into another, led to the discovery that certain very heavy elements could decay into lighter elements such as uranium decaying into lead. In the later 20th century, scientists documented tens of thousands of radiometric age measurements and that is how the earth was discovered to be billions of years old. So, what I am saying is what if these calculations are also wrong? Take the gap in our evolutionary record and man's jump forward. Man's intelligence over the past 100 years how quickly it changed from the wooden wheel to airplanes. So many things cannot be explained completely, such as the pyramids of Egypt and their builders. Then there is the big bang that started life. What if it wasn't such a bang?

The earth itself gains about 40,000 tons of cosmic dust every year, and the Sahara is the largest source of atmospheric dust, with 5 billion tons of dust particles transmitted throughout the earth every year. The surface has been collecting dust for billions of years so what is buried deep beneath? Could there be proof buried so deep that we haven't found it yet? Also, take into account how bones decay, maybe previous bones have already turned to dust. Is it then possible that people could have existed before and we will never find evidence? Did something happen to the earth, which killed all things; animals, plants, humans, even micros? Something like what we believed killed the dinosaur but was worse. Then Earth had to in essence reboot and start again and like before it started with the smallest of micros of life. We are discovering new information about the earth and life every day and as you know some contradict what is alleged and have been proven before, and I say proven with skepticism. With our ever-changing technology, we are establishing new ways to calculate ancient information better.

I want to induce you to think out of the box, so to say, and into coming up with new thoughts on how these things are possible and then finding a way to prove it. So, I put it out there for you to look around and question what you can determine as fact versus possible mistakes or lack of evidence. Do not dismiss questions because no answer exists, now dig, find, and resolve." The professor paused, then said, "That concludes today's lecture and I hope if I haven't opened your eyes, I have at least made you question human existence, and not believe everything that the preceding scientific community put forth."

Airy was now full of questions and wanted to talk to her professor more about this theory. "Dee, you go ahead I'll catch up to you at the apartment."

"I assumed we were going to get lunch before work tonight."

"Maybe later," she said, noticing Professor Morard already exited the auditorium doors. She made her way through a crowd of people just outside the entrance; not seeing her intended target, she made a path for Morard's office in the Archaeology department. She established a rapport with most of her instructors throughout her years at the university; however, she felt Professor Morard was her utmost supporter. She in turn liked him and enjoyed his classes along with the time she spent as his assistant the previous year. She knocked twice on the door. A voice beckoned her in.

"Hello Professor, I hope you had a few moments to clear up some questions I have about your lecture."

"Normally I would be delighted but I can't right now. Would you mind coming in tomorrow morning between eight to ten? I must catch a colleague from out of town right now; sorry I'm in a rush." He walked out the door with a briefcase in hand before she could reply.

Airy felt as though she was stranded on a desert island. Her thoughts rapidly flew threw her mind without any way to satisfy or expel them. She walked to her car and sent a text to Dee; after an eating place was established, she jotted down a few notes in her planner for tomorrow and left to meet her friend wondering if her day would hold on to the chaos that it began with.

Work exhausted every muscle that evening; and though she was looking forward to the party tonight with her friends she also dreaded, the late night she knew lingered before her. Hours later they were finally home and Airy helped her wasted roommate up the stairs to their apartment.

"Stop laughing so loud, Dee. You're going to wake the neighbors and you know how that Mrs. Seigh is, she will call the police just so the complex manager will have more ammo to throw us out. The last time you threw a party old man Wilson said he would evict us if we brought the police around again."

"Yeah, I know, Airy, but I can't stop he was just so funny looking with that big bush under his nose, and balding head. He spoke a California mix of surfer boy and Hispanic meets old dude." Dee nearly choked on the last words. The booze flowed freely tonight at their friend's 26th birthday party and she was blasted. She hadn't gotten this drunk in years, and it felt good just to let loose. She deliberated as she stumbled up the steps, with Airy supporting her every stride. To add to the night celebrations that old bushy mustache Uber driver was hitting on Airy, and true to her nature she politely thanked him for the compliments and turned any further conversation toward her away so he wouldn't think she had any interest in him, which she didn't. Not that her best friend wasn't into guys just that she was very choosy and didn't do any relationship casually.

"Dee, can you stand by yourself? I need to dig for my keys to open the door." Airy helped her friend propping her by the wooden doorframe as she rooted through her purse. Opening the door proved difficult when Dee began to slide down the frame toward the ground, but with Airy's help, she was standing again and they merged over the threshold. Once inside Airy quickly threw her purse and keys on the table and helped her friend to her room and bed. After a few more giggles, they said good night and Airy returned to lock the front door. Startled, she screamed, "Get out! What are you doing here? Get out now."

The man backed up and put his hands in the air. "Sorry, your friend forgot her purse in the back seat."

"That gives you no right to enter my home. Leave now!" Airy demanded.

"So sorry! I didn't mean anything coming in. It was just, you know, I noticed the door open some when I went to knock. Man, I'm sorry, Man, I was just going to sit the purse down on the couch and go. I didn't mean to frighten you," he said using the surfer-boy lingo again as he backed away toward the door.

"That's beside the point. You shouldn't have entered. I should report you."

"Please don't make a big deal out of this I was just trying to return her purse. Man, you can't even do a good deed nowadays," he stated as he pulled the door shut behind him.

Airy pondered for a second then rushed to the door and quickly deadbolted the lock then peered out the peephole. He scared her that was true, but it was also true that he tried to help by returning the purse. She considered going after him, thanking him, and apologizing for overacting but then thought better of it. He may be telling the truth or it was an excuse to gain access. Either way, she would be better off just sending Uber a note with a thank you, but no apology for her actions. It took a few minutes for Airy to calm herself before she made her way to her room and bed. She knew getting up in the morning for both herself and her roommate would be a chore; however, there wasn't an option for either girl to sleep in. Dee had classes and Airy wanted badly to keep her appointment with Professor Morard.

"Buzz, Buzz" went the alarm clock. Airy hastened to turn it off. Morning arrived too early, as she knew it would. She regretted drinking so much last night and was glad she didn't get as buzzed as Dee however, the boozes did leave her system feeling sluggish. Forcing herself from the warm covers, she moved on to the shower pulling back the brightly colored plastic curtain. As the warm water flowed over her body, Airy recalled the dream that she was having before the alarm awoke her sleeping form. Her grandfather came to her as she slept. She loved and missed him and found it hard to believe that he passed four years prior. He smiled at her as he always did with an award-winning grin which lit up her life as a child and continued throughout young adulthood. However, barely out of high school he passed on, she always felt like he was watching her and proud that she had chosen a field of study like his own. She recalled him reciting those same infernal numbers repeatedly asking her to remember them. She wondered why her dream was so vivid, so real, and why it had been all about numerals again, but now her grandfather was urging her to remember. As Airy lathered the blue liquid coconut soap over her body, she felt like these digits were to play a significant role in her life.

Airy arrived at Professor Morard's office at 8:30 that morning and the door was ajar with the interior light on. Hesitantly, she walked through the door. The professor was sitting at his desk with his laptop in front of him. Looking up as she entered, he said, "Ah, Airy, I am glad you came."

"Professor, I am eager to get you to clarify some thoughts I have about the theories you spoke of yesterday."

"Yes, I would enjoy that, but I have to ask you to do something very important first. You see I went to see an associate yesterday, and it seems as though a minor earthquake opened a crater in Africa a few weeks ago. Officials of that country have requested several scientists and a seismologist, along with a geologist, and I, an archaeologist with a paleontologist have been asked to descend into the hole. They want us to find out what is going on, right away; however, the university will not allow leave until I finish the semester. As you know, that is two more weeks and Africa wants someone there now. I would be pleased if you would go in my stead. I have cleared the temporary replacement and let them know whomever I choose would be worthy and has my respect. This person would stay to help me finish the project, once I arrive. I am confident this is perfectly suited for you; I dare say better than myself since the first part involves climbing down into the crater."

"Me?"

"Yes, you have a degree in archaeology with a minor in paleontology. You were my brightest student over the years as well as my aide for a year here at the university. I am convinced with your knowledge, and abilities in climbing; you are the most experienced person for this job. I will be there as soon as I tie up things here. Plus, I have talked to the paleontologist going, I have known him for years, and he has done extensive climbing so I know you will be in great hands. You think around the edge of the box so to say and he thinks outside the box so this increases the value of what you see and can determine from this expedition. Take notes on everything. However, there is something else I must tell you if you agree to do this."

Airy couldn't believe she decided so quickly to go to another continent and dangle from a rope not knowing the cavernous area she went to, and a downward scale was not at all her norm. Yes, she climbed with her father when he could get away from work, and her mom was always fearful when they did. Her mother hated them participating in anything that dangerous since she was terrified of heights but Airy and her father loved it. She loved the thrill and the accomplishment as well as the bonding experience it offered. But she hadn't done that in years and never more than 4164 meters like the summit of Breithorn in Switzerland.

Airy knew the reason she decided so quickly had to do only with the coordinates of the site. The fact that it would bring her closer to her career goal of becoming a real hands-on archaeologist was secondary.

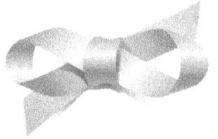

Chapter Two

Seth Lock sorted through his gear, taking note of everything he and his companion would need for an unknown hike and climb. He wasn't familiar with the area they were to go or the crater they were to enter. He didn't mind the unknown, for he was always able to adjust his mind and body to what lay ahead of him at that moment. However, this was a unique situation, and an unknown outcome lay ahead. He'd been a paleontologist for twelve years and went to several different countries excavating bones. Some digs were easy and others had him hanging off the side of a mountain with his tiny tools for hours on end, trying to extract bones from the clay and dirt. He enjoyed the rush, but not all the time it took. So, after some deep deliberation about work and other life items, he put that existence in the past and put his tiny tools away; for the past two years, he had been building homes with a team of men and women who like himself wanted to help others. They build homes for people with little to nothing, disabled, as well as veterans; the projects were funded by nonprofit organizations. He felt satisfied with his decision, until Morard's call. He was a friend, a colleague, and most importantly, he was his Uncle Stephen, and he needed his help.

• • ⚜ • •

"AIRY, YOU CAN'T JUST quit your job waitressing; the university probably doesn't pay enough for you to make your half of the rent, your car note, student loans, and other bills."

"No, but Professor Morard said that the African officials will be paying us and I am to get half of what he is to make, and believe me it's enough to pay for the next six months of rent and the other things."

"But why you, you have never done field research by yourself."

"I have done some with several different professors while getting my degree. This is my genuine chance to become an archaeologist, the field I have a degree in and I love. I have filled out more than 20 applications over the past two years for fieldwork with well-known members of the archaeology community and have not received anything more than an interest letter. Besides that, I need to go; I just feel this is somehow calling me. I can't explain it." Airy knew she could give enlightenment to a little part, but it wasn't logical to anyone other than herself.

"Airy, you aren't making sense, what do you mean, calling you?"

"Look Dee, I am going and there is nothing that you or anyone can say to keep me here. How about you be my friend and give me a lift to the airport."

"Sure, I can do that. While you're gone can I use your car if mine breaks down again?"

"Yes, my keys are on the nightstand in my room. Hey, only if yours breaks down or you wreck it again, okay."

. . ⚓ . .

"SEAT C18 IS ON THE left and is the outer seat, Miss Sheppard, and thank you for flying Shelton Airlines."

"Thank you." Airy made her way to her seat as other passengers followed suit. She placed her phone in her purse before she opened the compartment above the seats and placed it along with her small case that held her laptop and a few tools and essentials she felt she would need while in Africa. Her larger suitcase was checked in before boarding and would make the trip in the belly of the plane. Airy sat down and waited anxiously for the plane to fill.

She looked at the entrance several times for Morard's colleague hoping he would be like her professor, a man she respected. With anxiety getting, the better of her, she decided to open the book, she bought at the gift shop before boarding. After reading the first page twice and staring at the second unexpectedly a man stood over her, blocking the light, and began putting his bags in the overhead compartment.

When he was finished, he looked down and said, "Do you mind switching seats I feel locked in by the window?"

Airy stood and moved into the seat beside her, and asked, "Are you Professor Morard's colleague? When he requested me, I felt such excited that I didn't ask for his colleague's name."

"Yes, that would be me, may I assume you are his assistant."

"Yes, well, I was his student three years ago and his aide last year I occasionally sit in on lectures now." She raised her hand to shake his, "Airy Sheppard, Archaeologist, and I hold a minor degree in paleontology."

"Nice to meet you, Miss Sheppard Archaeologist, and minor Paleontologist, I am Seth Lock," he took her outstretched hand and a static spark went through them.

"Dr. Morard said you would brief me more as to this project and the expectations of the African government."

"Yes, in a few," he pulled out his phone and began typing out a message and after several return texts, he placed it back in his pocket and adjusted his seat. He wondered why his uncle would saddle him with a young inexperienced girl even if she had two degrees; she didn't have field experience. She didn't have enough experience in his eyes to be of use but since his uncle deemed her the best choice, he would do his best to put up with her.

Airy felt rejected because of his dismissing tone and she thought him arrogant and young compared to her mentor, also something unexpected an attraction of some sort to the handsome dark-haired man seated next to her. She tried her best not to let his tone rile her. She was certain he didn't intend to be condescending toward her since they only just met. She tried to put his negative response toward her out of her mind and concentrate on her book so as not to disturb him and create any further problems, but she hated men who thought themselves better just because they have a Y chromosome.

The flight attendant's voice came over the speaker and announced that the flight would start soon; she continued with safety information and said to turn off all cell phones and computers and to buckle the seat belts like so.

Airy's companion placed the seatbelt around his waist, and with a snap, it buckled. The engine roared and he asked looking straight in front of him, "So this is your first time going to Africa and Monrovia?"

"Yes." There was that condescending tone again and she wanted to yell at him, or slug him and make him stop treating her as if she was unimportant.

"The central areas can be dangerous with so many military and political agendas. I suggest after we depart the plane, you keep your eyes towards the ground when you see anyone with a military outfit on especially when we are traveling to other areas. This whole area is a little behind the times and they don't think much of women there; they are very disrespectful and have even captured women for pleasure. I am not saying this to be cruel, but I think you should be discerning and make sure you don't talk back to any of them. We should be clear of the region where that sort of thing happens regularly, but I think caution would be wise. And just so you are aware once we get there, I will be carrying a handgun for protection. Can you shoot?"

Airy's anger for his patronizing attitude was beginning to swarm and she almost threw the book in her hand at him letting him know she was perfectly capable of taking care of herself and knew how to act in dangerous circumstances so he didn't have to treat her like a fragile child. Since this was their first meeting she didn't want to start on the wrong footing, so she held back. "I have fired rifles before. I am aware of the civil turbulence and the monstrous thing that has gone on, but I was assured we wouldn't be in that area however in the event of uncertainnness I will do what is best."

"As I said we shouldn't, but that doesn't mean trouble won't find us."

"I see, thank you for advising me and I will be visual while we are there."

"Good. Better safe, than sorry."

The plane started to taxi down the runway, picking up speed as it went. Within seconds, the nose went upwards and as the body lifted off the ground, they endured a lurch forward then the plane zoomed into the air.

"That was a smooth take-off, I wish they all could be that way," Seth said with a jovial smile.

"I don't mind most take-offs but when we hit high-level turbulence that can bring on anxiety."

"I suppose now's a good time as any to give you more about our little expedition."

"Yes, I would like that; Professor Morard told me little other than some coordinates and that a disturbance was caused by an earthquake." She still didn't care for his brashness with her but at least he was now trying to be more pleasant.

"That is true, though what we still don't understand is why in this particular area. You see Mt. Nimba is part of West Africa and is not seismically active like the eastern side. The region is 1,752 meters in altitude and is a Nature Reserve located on the borders of Guinea, Liberia, and Cote D'lvoire. It is composed of dense forest at the foot, slopes, and grassy mountain pastures. But for us, I suppose the most interesting factor is the coordinates of Mt. Nimba also known as Mount Richard Monlard 7.6167 degrees north and 8.4167 degrees west."

"Yes, I must admit that is what initiated my curiosity, that and the amazing chance to gain experience in the field."

"So why do you feel Stephen considered you qualified for this expedition?"

"He stated he has confidence in my knowledge of archaeology and paleontology that and my capacity to think around the edge of the box would complement your ability to think outside. Also, climbing would be involved and I have experience in that field as well. I am proficient in martial arts gaining my blackbelt at age twelve and since I have become a fourth-degree blackbelt." She hoped that would help him not judge someone beforehand.

"Well, I hope you live up to your hype."

"I can assure you, Mr. Lock, you will consider me quite versed in all areas."

"Well, one thing we must do is drop the formalities, call me Seth and may I call you, Airy?"

"Yes, that's fine."

"Where did you receive such an unusual name?"

"My parents said that when I first arrived, nearly a month premature, they hadn't settled on a name. So, they started looking in the baby's name book, which my mother carried in her purse, and as soon as she saw the name and its meaning instantly thought it was a perfect fit for the screaming baby, she'd just birthed."

"Do tell."

"She explained that the first words she read were, 'boss figure doesn't like to take orders, mysterious, independent, confident, freethinker, creative but loves to lead, curious, and impetuous,' all these qualities she loved the idea of her little girl having."

"Okay, so that gives me an idea of what I am in for on this trip. I guess I will get the chance to see if you live up to your name," Seth smiled.

For the first time, Airy looked at the man who sat beside her. His skin tanned to a bronze color and he possessed dark brown eyes with long lashes. Not as long as a woman's, however, they were lengthy for a man. His face was kindly looking. His smile dazzled when the corners of his mouth raised, and his lips plump red that showed slightly under his brown mustache and above his goatee-type beard, which was the same chocolate color as his hair. She suddenly wanted to kiss his red lips and wondered if the goatee or mustache would tickle as they kissed.

Leaning his chair back, he asked, "Is there anything else I can assist you with before I try for a nap?"

"No," she nearly screamed, and recovering quickly she added, "What do you make out about the coordinates?"

"What do you mean?"

"Well didn't the professor tell you that the numbers were popping up all over the world as of late?"

"He mentioned something to that nature, probably just coincidence."

"He said even news reports contained that particular combination in most instances, and people winning the lottery with the same combo, but millions instead of thousands of instances where people noticed those numbers in everyday life and only in the last two years."

"You feel it has to do with fate or something of an impractical nature?"

"Maybe, I don't know but it seems strange, I even dreamt of those figures," Oh, why had she voiced that she wondered.

"So, you are one of them, a believer."

"What? What's a believer?"

"Oh, just what people are starting to be called for thinking the numbers have more to do with something extraordinary than just simply being numbers. They feel that they are a message."

"A message? A message from whom?" she wanted to know.

"To the people of the earth," his mind flashed back to a dream he had as a teen with his buddy and he quickly shook his head putting the thought aside.

"What, are you talking about aliens from outer space?" she gave a little questioning giggle.

"It is the rumor," he stated.

"How come I haven't heard of this?"

"Well, it's talked about in the scientific community as well as your alien theorist on the web."

"I assume I am in the dark then."

"You don't use the web?" he looked at her curiously.

"Yes, of course, I do, but only when needed. My job, the university, and keeping up with looking for an expedition group or any article that concerns my degree where I can find work, keep me rather busy. Applications to expeditions take so long to fill out when I do find one, first your life story, then degree facts, and then start the questions and quizzes to see if they like your answers. I've been on a few excavations while working toward my degree, but no employment since receiving them. You?"

"Straight out I got my first gig and we found a Daspletosaurus horneri and continued nonstop, then I started getting funded for my own in which I found an ancient vulture-like eagle in Australia called Cryptogyps Aquila audacious," he discontinued before telling her that he wasn't working as a paleontologist anymore."

"Lucky you," Her aggravation surfaced to the fact as she saw more men were hired for digs than females, and in both fields, they excavate for history just his relied on bone fossils and hers were tools and other useful human historical items. The reason she minored in paleontology was she liked the hunt and tools and fossil evidence were the same to her. In both fields, you must be careful with your items and in studying both fields, you needed to know about the past, people, as well as animals so it seemed logical to embark upon both fields of study.

Her degree took her on a longer path but only by several years, and most students approach that time because they can't decide on a major, whereas she knew hers going in.

    Moments went by, as both parties were deep in thought; however, Seth hadn't missed her sarcastic comment, though he refused to acknowledge knowing what she meant and it was true. He'd lived a charmed existence, his family was well off, he'd made a name in his chosen profession, and to top it off, he now working with a charity and still profited from his former and his new occupations. He placed a ball cap on his head and issued a blank statement, "You should think about your life, and create your own results."

    "What do you mean?"

    "Shhh, think about it," he shifted in the seat and turned away from her. Placing the cap low on his brow to block out the light, and then placing the headphones in front of him over his ears, he said out loud, "Time to sleep."

.

    Airy pondered what he meant by creating her own results and after several attempts to question him; she was met with a light snore from the still form in the seat beside her. She tried to read her book again, but it held no interest and her mind continuously replayed what her companion said driving her to the point of insanity so she placed the book in her striped oversized bag reclined her seat slightly, and looked out the window.

    . . ⚭ . .

THE PLANE ROCKED A few times managing to wake any sleeping passengers, and then a man's voice came over the speaker, "Sorry folks, for the turbulence but we are just breaking through a small storm. Don't fret although we do ask you to buckle your seat belts and place your chairs upright for safety. Just then, they hit another pocket and they were jolted forward in their seats, a few whimpers and ahhs were heard throughout the plane. Airy grabbed the seat armrest and white-knuckled it. Her throat grew taut as she silently said a little prayer for safety. She wasn't much for religion even though she did grow up in the Catholic faith and those early teachings stuck with her, even if barely used anymore. Again, they were pitched back and forth and up and down as if on an ocean. There was a loud pop and someone screamed, 'Lightening hit the plane.' Airy looked outside as did most passengers. She could feel Seth's hot breath on the back of her neck as he strained to look past her.

"I don't see anything, do you, Airy?"

"No, nothing."

The plane was riding normally again and the other passengers appeared to calm now discerning no lightning hit the plane or at least didn't do any real damage. Several minutes passed, with no added occurrences, so the people on board sat back in their seats and conversation began again as the flight continued as normal.

Unlike her partner, Airy was unable to rest while the flight continued. Her apprehension of the air travel and storm they went through, along with her anticipation conjured up all kinds of scenarios that they were to embark on. When at last exhaustion did overtake Airy's dreams plagued her, until the pilot and the jolting plane interrupted bringing her upright in her chair. She looked around as the announcement came over the speaker. No one seemed panicked, most were like herself just waking up, and a few were reading books or watching the movie that played on the screen in their section. Still others like her partner were viewing computer tablets which only recently were allowed on during flights.

Straightening her golden hair with her fingers, she spoke to Seth, "Is everything okay? Is the plane all right?"

"Yes, just a little more turbulence however the pilot did say we picked up a tailwind and would be arriving earlier than expected." He never looked away from the tablet's screen.

"What's so interesting?" she wanted to know.

"I was just going over some notes about our assignment and making a few additions on things we will need for the trip."

"Would you like me to review the list, I may think of something you haven't, after all your needs as a paleontologist and mine as an archeologist are different and I may have other needs as well."

"Sure, add anything you like. I plan to make this trip as quick and efficient as possible," he handed her the tablet.

Reading through the list twice she made only a few other additions and subtractions, then handed it back to him, "You did a great job of satisfying both our needs from what I see. I brought my own tool set so I marked out a few you listed; hope that's okay, we can both use the items of mine I took off."

Seth looked at the list again and noticed the removals so it didn't upset his requirements and he further observed the few, female comforts she added to the list; it made him smile slightly because she added a second tent letting him know she didn't plan to share. He should have realized that, but he'd never accommodated a female on his digs, mostly because it was usually only himself and a fellow member or an entire crew and someone else was taking care of all those kinds of items. He considered once more, just how inexperienced in the field she was and wondered again if she may be more of a hindrance to this operation. He respected his uncle and decided that everyone must start somewhere, but why did he have to be the one babysitting a newbie?

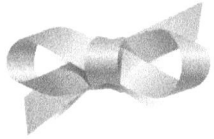

Chapter Three

The flight attendant stood and took the microphone from the wall; she blew slightly into it and started her announcements over the speaker. "Please turn off any electronics and seatbelts must be buckled, place all seats and trays in the upright position for the final approach to land. We hope your flight was enjoyable and please fly Shelton Airlines again soon." She then placed the mic back on the hanger, sat down in front of her passengers, and buckled her seatbelt.

The plane made a smooth landing twenty minutes later. After a five-minute wait, it taxied up to the airport and all passengers departed. Seth and Airy were the last to proceed off. Once in the airport, they retrieved their luggage and made their way to the adjacent hotel where Seth checked them both in at the desk. Going to the elevator he pushed the button for the second floor. When they exited, he walked Airy to her room unlocked her door, and said as he helped her inside, "Take some time to clean up and rest while I find our guide, I will meet you in the hotel restaurant about 8:30 and we will go over everything then."

"If you need help making arrangements and gathering the supplies, I can rest later."

"No, that's quite okay I can handle everything," he turned and went to his room to drop off his luggage.

Again, he made her feel like she wasn't useful to this project. Airy felt strange now that they landed. Looking around the room the nervousness that plagued her ever since Professor Morard asked her to go to Africa, became overbearing. Her sights settled on the adjoining door. Did Mr. Lock ask for a room with an adjoining door or was this normal for this hotel, she wondered. The thought that he might want something more from her made her feel unsteady and she sat on the bed quickly, her legs feeling like liquid. As she sat trembling it occurred to her that before the plane Seth didn't even know her and therefore, he couldn't have requested the room to be adjoining. He is not here to come on to you, and you are here to work, she scolded herself. She put further quires out of her mind, went to the bathroom, and started a relaxing bath, something to soothe her mind. Airy, lay there in the hot water enjoying the sanctuary of the room knowing that they would soon be in tents sleeping on the ground, with no restrooms or tubs for the next few days to weeks or maybe even more. Airy wondered if she was up for such a demanding event. She hoped so because there was no backing out now.

· · ✧ · ·

AT PRECISELY 8:30, Airy walked into the hotel's elegant restaurant. She didn't pack anything fancy to wear however; she did pack a black long skirt and a white cotton V-neck lightweight sweater and added a wide belt to dress up the outfit. Her mother taught her to always be prepared. Her black hiking boots were barely noticeable underneath the simple but stylish ensemble.

Seth looked up as she leisurely walked into the room. Her long hair of spun gold was pulled back and tied with a black satin ribbon, and a slim waist accented with a zebra print belt. Seth felt his Adam's apple go up and down as he watched her walk toward him. He didn't notice until that moment how very beautiful she was, and as she crossed the distance to him, his body rose from the chair to pull hers out before reseating himself. He looked across the table unsure how to act.

"I hope I didn't keep you waiting," she knew she was on time but at the frozen look on his face, she didn't know what else to say.

"No, you're right on time, would you like a glass of wine?"

"No, I seldom drink alcohol, water is fine."

The waitress came to the table, sat two menus down, and asked for their drink order. Seth spoke up, "A glass of ice water for the lady and I will have a beer, any on tap is fine." He felt as though he needed something strong; he normally drank water also but tonight somehow felt more like a date than a meeting however, he had no idea why.

"Were you able to gather everything for our leave in the morning?"

"Yes, our guide will meet us outside the hotel and he has hired a few hands to help with equipment and the dig. They will be armed in case an incident of danger arises. You did bring pants for the dig?"

What did he mean by asking if she brought pants of course she did, he must think she wasn't adept for the expedition. "As I told you before I am qualified for this job so yes, I did pack practical wear," she ended the statement with a huff.

Seth had to be certain and the only way to find out was to ask, he couldn't very well wait for tomorrow to see if she was prepared. He was in charge of this excavation and it is essential she respected that actuality, and with her little searing proclamation, he wasn't sure she realized that fact. "I recognize that may be an insensitive question, making you think I feel you lack the ability to know what is required, but try and see my perspective. I am tasked with making sure everyone and everything goes off without a glitch and if any member of this crew is not capable in every way, then that reflects on me as the captain of this expedition. In all fairness, I don't know you and though I assume you are prepared, it's my job to be positive. I hope you understand my position as the leader for the American side of this project, though if it makes you feel any better once we are on the site I will not be fully in charge." He hoped that put her at ease solidifying that he was in charge for now and she needed to abide by that detail.

Airy realized he was correct of course but he didn't have to belittler her and she felt like that is what his question and explanation did. "You are in charge and I will make sure I pull back my reaction to allow a cohesive working relationship, boss," she added the boss with a slight giggle to lighten to mood.

Her eyes were a lovely shade of pale green and he felt drawn into them when she smiled. He didn't think he noticed before what a lovely smile she possessed. How the corners of her mouth curved upward in an upside-down v shape. Though he did notice her trim waist and small breasts earlier, he didn't let himself take any pleasure in her form as his mind focused on the business ahead. However, now as she giggled and grinned, he permitted himself to gaze at the woman across from him and become aware of all her attributes, of which he now discovered there were many. "We will have plenty of time on the way to Mt. Nimba to discuss the excavation, so for tonight how about we get to know each other better so we perhaps will have a better working alliance?"

They concluded dinner nearly an hour later having shared a few stories of their past. Airy talked about her father and grandfather mostly and her dreams about the coordinates; Seth shared some information about his parents as well as how he left his field of study and was now building homes for the less fortunate.

Seth paid the bill with his visa card and put the receipt in his wallet. Airy offered to give compensation for her part but he insisted that the group that hired them would cover it along with their supplies and the hotel. They decided before retiring for the evening to take a walk to look at the garden that stretched the length of the hotel. The gardens year-round host 29 different exquisite flowers in bloom. Some of the wonderful native floras were the Red-Hot Poker, Fire Lilies, and Gazania Rigens Daisy, which have a beautiful orange color with a black center. Cape Primrose in red, lined the outer edge of the walkway. The garden also supported many different types of grasses making the entire location a wondrous hub of natural beauty. The topic was casual as they walked around the area back to the doors that led them inside the hotel. With goodnights exchanged, they both retreated to their rooms in anticipation of the following morning.

A TRUCK WITH A CANOPY over the back pulled up in front of the hotel along with two army-type jeeps. The truck contained gear, food, and men armed with machine guns, along with men who looked like workers. In the second jeep, Seth and Airy climbed in and the troop of people made their way out of the busy town to a rural area before climbing upwards in the forest on dirt roads. As the men in Airy's SUV chatted, she listened to them talk of their surroundings and things that they could encounter on the journey toward Mt. Nimba.

As the men spoke, Airy learned that the reserves located around Mt. Nimba are seldom visited due to the entry is permission dependent, and is strictly regulated by responsible local authorities though they were entering on the Liberia side, Guinea was informed ahead so there wouldn't be any squabbling between countries. They also talked about dangerous wildlife like the West African Lion, and the African Golden Cat. There were also less harmless creatures such as the Zebra duiker, monkeys like Chimpanzees, and pygmy Hippopotami. Airy felt as though in a fantasy as she viewed the land. Mountain peaks lay in the distance and squawking monkeys sat in trees as the vehicles ascended the road.

She was closing in on her first real dig and she didn't even know if she would excavate because the only information, they were privy to was an earthquake opened a fissure and there was something that all scientists needed to examine. This fracture was at the coordinates that she and others dreamt of; and still, others have seen numbers appearing everywhere in daily life for more than two years. This phenomenon has been taking place around the globe in all communities including scientific ones. After what Dr. Morard said about others having some type of experience with these numbers this convinced her that she was important to this project. What could all this mean, why would something so strange happen to so many people? Why was she just now experiencing the coordinate phenomenon? She wondered still staring out as the mountainous terrain came clearer into view.

The ride thus far flowed smoothly however Airy noticed ahead the unpaved road looked more like a dry patch of grass than a road. She braced herself for the upcoming hazards that were likely to come, and moments later they did. She grabbed the roll bar as they slammed into the treacherous area. The jeep seemed to go downward with the dip they collided into, and as she adjusted herself in the seat, they hit another area that left her flying up only to return hard on her bottom. This terrain lasted for the rest of their ride that day until the vehicles stopped so the group could make camp for the night. Tomorrow would see them to the area where they would begin their climb on foot approaching the coordinates in question. As Airy placed the tent stakes into the hard earth she prayed the remaining trip wouldn't have as many bumps as today's because she was aching all over from the exertion of holding on and flying up and down.

"Do not be offended however with my tent in its place I wondered if you need any assistance with yours?" asked a familiar strong voice from behind.

"Thank you, but I am just finishing up."

"Okay, I am going to go over tomorrow's trek with Hector would you like to join us?" Seth questioned.

"Yes, kind of you to ask."

"This way," he said with his hand out before them.

They walked over to their guide who was standing beside his tent smoking a cigarette. When he noticed them, he threw the nub to the ground and stomped it out.

"We have come to see our route for tomorrow and once we are on foot," Seth spoke pleasantly to the man.

"Yes, come with me and I will get my maps and we can take a look." Hector laid them out on the hood of the jeep to view easily. Once there he explained pointing at a dot on the map, "The trip is mostly upward and the land is rough but won't have as many roughed dips as today." They were to spend another night before continuing onward and they were lucky because the trip on foot would likely only take a half day. His men will carry most of the gear so they will only have to worry about the trek itself.

Satisfied with the guide's explanation Seth thanked him and let Airy know that he preferred to bring her meals to her since she was the only woman in a camp of more than ten men, the less interaction the better for her.

"I don't mind eating with the others," she professed saddened to be by herself.

"No, I must insist. I remind you again we are in a foreign country and from what I do know of their different customs and beliefs; I would feel better for your safety. I just prefer we don't take chances. I have already heard talk from some about your . . . let's say appearance, and I would like your interaction to be limited. I hope you won't fight me on this at least until I get to know these men a little better. After tonight I would hope you set up your tent closer to mine so I can hear you if the need arises." He hoped his words didn't upset her but he didn't want anyone thinking that she was available in any way. With luck, these men are professional, and there won't be any trouble for either of them.

"I do understand what you mean and will do my best. However, I must question you about my appearance is it something that needs attention, are my clothing not loose enough or rugged enough?" she questioned holding her arms open wide.

"It is not that." How did he tell her she is beautiful and even in loose pants and shirt with that big floppy hat she is desirable to every man in camp? He wondered before he declared. "Men notice a woman and you, for lack of a better explanation, stick out like a fox in the hen house."

"Oh, I see. Is there anything different I can do?"

"Other than keep to yourself as much as possible."

"I am used to taking care of myself however I understand these circumstances are very different so I will do as you say." She hated backing down from any situation, especially one that could easily be handled. Though in the spirit of being cooperative, she would let Seth decree how he preferred these circumstances to be managed for now.

Seth walked away grateful for her acceptance and he also looked forward to the prospect of having another reason to interact with her later when he brought her meal.

・・ ⚘ ・・

THE GROUP ARRIVED AT the edge of the river they needed to cross. They stopped and prepared the trucks and teams for the excursion across the rapidly flowing rock-filled pool. The truck would cross first followed by first one jeep and then the other because they were prone to float. The second jeep held Airy and Seth. Four men were to be on the banks holding ropes tied to trees in case a vehicle began to flow with the water before making their way through. The guide Hector and two others went in the first jeep which did float a little way before wheeling its way out onto the other side.

Airy held on to the frame of their jeep as they slowly moved forward. The vehicle lurched to the right as it hit a rock on the left before leveling out again. They made it to the middle with only a few more tilts of the small truck, and just as Airy felt things were going well, she loosened her grip, though that was a fatal error in judgment because the jeep went to the left and water poured in as it lurched forward and nearly flipped over. Her fingers were throbbing holding on as tight as she could, and where Seth held her, her arm felt like the skin torn from the bone. The little SUV wrenched again and twisted her arm as her fingers peeled off. Her foot slipped and before she could catch herself, the water pulled her body out and into the rushing river.

As her body went through the opening Seth grabbed for her but the water outside rushed past towing her with it.

With extreme velocity, her body raced through the river. She went beneath the cold liquid and came up coughing numerous times. Her legs and arms hit rocks as her body whipped through the rushing water with a hard crash, she felt her head explode with pain, and then everything went dark.

Seth jumped over the edge of the open-roofed vehicle. He swam with the swiftly flowing water toward Airy as her body fiercely fought the gushing fluid around her. He saw her go under and her body seemed to go limp before him. With adrenaline pumping, he pushed himself to get to her in time. He seized her leg and then arm and began dragging her with great effort toward the rocky shore fighting the rushing water as they went.

With ragged breaths, he positioned her on the sand and questioned, "Are you okay? Airy? Airy, say something?" there was no response. Seth tilted her head and began CPR. Moments later a semi-conscious Airy began to spit up water choking on the liquid. Seth sat back on his heels; dripping water fell from his dark hair into his eyes and with a quick swoop of his forearm, he wiped it away. "You scared the life out of me," he said at last.

Still sputtering she responded, "Yeah, let's make it's all about you."

His brown eyes brightened; there was the young woman he was getting to know and like, touches of sarcasm even when she nearly died. But her attitude washed relief over him and that is all he needed to know that she was well, "How about we continue with this trip but in a vehicle this time."

She smiled a half smile nodding while Seth stood up, and put out his hand to help her stand. They walked quite away to rejoin the others who were already making their way toward the couple.

Hector came running up to them first, "Are you two all right?"

"Yeah, just a little excitement is all. How's everyone else?"

"Fine. We managed to pull the jeep to shore, no worse for wear."

"If you want, we can set up camp and carry on tomorrow?"

He glanced quickly in Airy's direction however, he knew what she thought before he did so, "Thanks but if it's all the same to everyone we would like to continue."

With wet clothing, they climbed into the jeep with Hector and when the truck pitched forward Airy grabbed the roll bar quickly. Seth couldn't help the smirking sound that left his throat.

The sun overhead baked their bodies and dried their wet clothing. Airy rode quietly most of the remaining day. Her mind was not only on the accident hours earlier that nearly took her life but also on how her life changed in mere days. Never would she have dreamt that she would be in Africa, let alone on an expedition for some unknown, or an artifact, or what she didn't have a clue lay ahead of them; though she knew whatever it was she would be safe in Seth's capable company as they searched.

. . ∽ . .

THE DAY STARTED WITH a hearty breakfast cooked by Eli the large man that wasn't only a cook, but also one of the men hired to protect them. Once all the items were packed, they started the hike up the mountain, which proved too steep for vehicles. One man stayed behind to guard the trucks so they would have a way back to Monrovia.

The sun beamed down all day but the temperatures this time of year maxed out at 78 degrees so the heat for the climb wasn't difficult although the ascent itself did consist of hindrances such as vines, shrubs, rocks, steeps, and dusty terrain.

Airy enjoyed the fresh air as they made their way upward. Her contentment surfaced in this nature-saturated area, with all its wildlife and beauty that surrounded them. She stopped once to watch some monkeys in a tree swing to the next or just groom their neighbor. She also took pleasure in the white clouds overhead, the wildflowers, the green grasses, the numerous trees, and the splendor that surrounded them. She wished it were possible to build a home up here on the mountain and walk out onto this majestic land every day and let the breeze filter through her body. It was magnificent and she knew only a few would have the satisfaction of ever experiencing it, and if not for the accident in the river yesterday she likely wouldn't have noticed its splendor today. She contemplated a minute on how funny it was that no one took notice of the earth's beauty or life and its miracles until a terrifying experience.

"What are you thinking about?" Seth questioned startling her.

"Nothing really, just this place is stunning, with all the colors, some so deep and rich I think I've never seen such lushness before in nature."

"Yes, I think it's due to the temperatures that are fairly constant most of the year."

"Whatever, I am inclined to bottle it up and take it home," she smiled.

"I'll see what I can do to make that happen," Seth, jest. "I just wanted to tell you we only need to make the hill to be there," he pointed to a peak."

"Finally, we will get to see what all the fuss has been about," she felt anxious now.

"Yes, and tomorrow we will begin work," he said feeling enthused that they were at last nearing their destination.

The area proved to be the most challenging part of their journey, with its almost straight-up incline, and stony terrain but ultimately, they were there, and while most made camp, others began the task of unpacking the equipment that was purchased to make the stay more hospitable.

Airy made short work of putting up her tent in anticipation of their assignment and all the unknowns ahead. She noticed Seth talking with Hector over near the small cabin-like building, and to his left, there were four men, she didn't recognize with riffles and she knew that they had not come with them. There were also four more men joining them that she didn't recognize. Airy began to wonder why they were there, if this task was more dangerous in a way she'd never thought of before, or if they were guarding something of more importance than perceived. She wanted to know now what was going on but consider the advice Seth gave her about maintaining a low key and not making any moves that attracted attention to her, and she theorized that going into a huddle of men demanding answers would do just that.

Thirty minutes later and with no sign of the men ending whatever was going on, Airy decided to go inside her tent. She opened her clothing bag to gather the pants and shirt she usually put on to sleep. She took her water bottle and a washrag and poured water on it then wiped her face, neck, and arms; she then reached out her tent squeezing the water and dirt out of the cloth before placing it back in her bag. When she finished, she noticed she'd taken out her cell phone accidentally and curiosity made her turn it on and check the reception. There was none but that didn't surprise her since she hadn't seen any cell towers in days. Turning it off she placed it in her bag and zipped it up. Just then, she heard Seth call her name outside her tent. Jumping to her feet, she went through the flap in a rush. "Yes?"

"Hi, I hope I didn't disturb you but I have some news."

She stood apprehensively waiting for him to continue.

"We are not allowed to begin until tomorrow; however, we are permitted to go see where we will be working. We will have to descend to the area where we are to begin so for safety reasons we can't work at night."

"I understand, but why bother going to see the area tonight? Why not wait?"

"From what I was told it is best to wait until dark to see the area and witness what made this entire expedition necessary."

"That doesn't make sense. How are we to see in the dark?"

"I can only give information I have."

"Why are there guards already here?"

"They are here to protect the area and keep anyone out except those invited by the government."

"Oh, I questioned if we were in mortal danger or something with so many military men," she stated with relief washing across her face making her eyes brighten.

Seth noticed the flash of light beaming off her now deep green eyes and felt himself swallow hard. "Well to be truthful it seems that word has gotten out about the potential importance of this area and just last week they fought a group of men trying to see what they could collect. They most likely thought diamonds or gold was discovered."

"So how did they get them to leave?"

"The men did what they were trained for," he said a little saddened by the actions that transpire.

"No! They were killed?"

Chapter Four

"Like I said, they did what was needed when the men wouldn't leave and decided to rush them. They defended themselves and the location. I know this all seems bizarre to you but in areas like this and for something that has the potential to be astonishing the government must maintain authority in any way possible."

"But to murder."

"Well, I don't believe the government thinks of it as murder, it is more like safeguarding their property."

"Are we safe, they won't hurt us if they don't like what we do will they?"

Seth laughed, "You forget we were invited to participate in this expedition. They will make sure no harm comes to us while we are here, just as the men who came with us. Now let's go get some grub before it is devoured by all our guards."

Night arrived none too soon for Airy. She gathered her battery-powered headlamp and walked over to the group of men, and the deep voice that she was now familiar with welcomed her. She thought how strange it was that Seth no longer seemed like a stranger, though she still thought of him as arrogant. "Let's get this show on the road," she spoke enthusiastically, more to Seth than the rest as she entered the circle.

He smiled smugly and proclaimed, "I was just expressing those same thoughts. Shall we go look at this amazing area gentlemen?"

One of the military men swung his gun over his shoulder and declared, "This way gentlemen, and ladies."

Airy wondered why he would say, ladies. Looking around she noticed no one at first and then she took in the appearance of one of the people who wore fatigues. There was a slimmer person within the cluster and she could see a hit of the shape beneath the shirt as they began to walk, a shape much like hers. So, she wasn't alone up here with only men after all. She smiled to herself gratified to have another person to commune with in the middle of a sea of men.

Seth tapped her shoulder, "Ready?"

"Oh, yes let's."

They walked together with chatter all around them. It took only about five minutes or so before the officer turned to the group, his headlight blazing in their eyes, and stated, "We have arrived. Please be very careful because the crater opening is ahead and has a very steep grade and though we will not be going down tonight if you don't watch your step you could fall over the edge. I am afraid if that happens, we won't find your crumpled body till morning. Does everyone understand? Also, don't lean into the ropes they can give way. The lights around the area are hooked up to a generator so be careful of the cords we wouldn't want to lose the lights that keep you from falling inside." He spoke loudly, because of the noise the generators were putting off.

Airy looked at Seth with wide eyes, and they both smiled. The pair was elated to finally see what all the fuss was in relationship to. The group walked up to the edge looking carefully over the rim beyond the string of lighting. It was nothing short of magnificent and they stood in awe transfixed by the blue, pink, and yellow glow that came out of the side of the mountain within the depression. The light seemed to pulse in a rhythm every thirty seconds.

"What is it?" Airy asked of Seth.

"I don't know maybe something geological."

"That is certainly possible." A heavily laced English voice came from beside Seth interrupting. "I am sorry but we have not been introduced as of yet. I am Doctor Sonya Ramsey, I am a geoscientist or geologist whichever you prefer from Rwanda, I arrived two days ago and have been studying the lights from up here. I don't believe them to be any kind of reflective or refractive rock and I know none that can make the light come from it such as that. Though quartz crystals, such as amethyst are reflective and refracted the glow can be two hues or as a rainbow; however, it would need light to respond as such. Rocks that glow usually need ultraviolet light. You are the archaeologist and paleontologist that were flown in from the US, is that correct?"

"Yes, that is us," Seth answered. "Do you have any theories as of yet?"

"Not really. Mostly I have ruled out ideas, but my work like yours has just started. I will be descending with you tomorrow since I am the only other scientist here with that capability." She spoke in a much lower tone, "The others are old men, and they have already retired for the evening."

"Well then it is up to us to have all the fun," Airy let out a little giggle.

"Yes, and we will need to be very cautious as we trek down; the ground is believed to be unstable and could shift."

"Yes, caution is wise," Seth chimed in. "I am Seth Lock Paleontologist and this is Airy Sheppard she is the archeologist for this project."

Smiling at Airy Sonya said, "Nice to have another female around with a group of brutes."

"Are they really brutes?"

"No, most have been extremely nice and welcoming to me. There is one that I would say to try to stay out of his path. His mates call him Dex. He gives off bad vibes and he watches from afar, so stay clear if you can."

The military officer interrupted announcing it was time to walk back to camp; tomorrow all personnel could resume their research. He turned and led the way observing that no one stayed behind. The two armed guards in the rear would make certain protocol was accepted.

Once at camp Sonya said goodnight and made her way to the other side of the encampment. Seth walked Airy to her tent and also said goodnight and reminded her that they would need to be up early to start. Airy knew she wouldn't get much sleep tonight and asked Seth, "What are you thinking we should do first tomorrow?"

"I plan to have a good breakfast," he stated jovially.

"Very funny, you know what I mean."

"I think we need to be certain the area is safe before we descend to the specific origin of the anomaly."

"I suppose you're right, but I just want to dive in."

"Patience, we will get there. Safety before all else agreed."

"Yes, though there is something I should tell you about myself."

"What's that?"

"Patience and I do not go well together."

"Nice to know."

"One last thing."

"Yes?" he smiled.

"I love surprises and I think this one is going to be glorious."

"I believe you may be right, now go and get some rest."

"Fine, I will give it my all," Airy opened the flap to her tent and slipped inside.

Pushing the tiny button on her watch to illuminate the numbers in the dark tent with its white light, the time flashed 3:00, it was the fourth time she looked at her watch and it still wasn't morning. Until this point, she didn't think she'd obtained more than an hour of sleep. Her mind couldn't rest, she thought of the light and the crater, the earthquake that brought about the crater and the numbers that continued to plague her mind and keep rest at bay. Nothing about this made sense, the numbers, and the coordinates being the same which was the most baffling. Who noticed the first link to people and the reoccurring numbers, and who figured out they were coordinates to here; and were they assumed before the earthquake that there was a connection taking place? What if anything did it have to do with her dreams of her grandfather? Was it alien? All these questions plagued Airy making it impossible to shut down. She felt tingling as if electricity was surging through her. Sleep would not happen tonight and normally she would research online or go make a soothing cup of hot tea. Though here there was no internet, no cell phone capabilities, and no way for her to leave the safety of her tent at night.

Morning brought a somewhat grumpy Airy to life. Her eyes fluttered open to the dim morning rays; stretching her arms above her head and pushing her legs out to their full length she tried to rouse herself. Sleeping on the ground wasn't nearly as fun as she remembered it being, but at last, it was morning and they would finally begin their examination of the area and hopefully soon the point of light. With those thoughts, she quickly dressed for the day and made her way outside the tent. Men were milling around and she wondered if Seth was still asleep since she didn't see him. His tent was next to hers so she took a few steps and said, "Seth, are you awake?" No answer met her so in a louder voice she questioned again, "Seth, are you awake?"

"Yes," he said behind her.

Airy jumped and spun around, "What the Hell?"

"Sorry, did I frighten you?"

"What do you think?" she said with irritation lacing her words.

"Here's a peace offering," he handed her a cup of coffee and said, "Breakfast is ready shall we go get it before there is none left?"

Gratefully she accepted his attempt to appease her, and begrudgingly voiced her thanks and answered, "Yes, food would be nice."

Dr. Ramsey was at the outside table already eating as they approached, "Please join us," she waved Airy and Seth toward her.

"I would like to introduce you to Dr. Abraham Kellser in charge of physics; Dr. Marc Semen is our chemist."

"Nice to meet everyone I am Seth Lock Paleontologist, and this is Airy Sheppard Archeologist, we look forward to an excellent collaboration. I hope to hear your theories so far gentlemen."

They both nodded and took another bite of their meal barely acknowledging the newcomers. Seth wasn't insulted, he understood older men were set in their ways and looked at the younger generation as inter-loafers, and he hoped at that age he wouldn't be so cynical of the younger crowd. Though as he looked at Airy, he could see it disturbed her to be treated with annoyance. He placed his hand on the small of her back directing her to take a seat by Sonya and he moved to seat himself across from her. "So, Dr. Ramsey, I'd like to start with the area's surroundings this morning, you will be coming along, correct?"

"Yes, I have my climbing gear prepared when you and Miss Sheppard are ready."

"Great. Gentlemen, will either of you be joining us?"

They both answered in unison, "No." Then Dr. Semen said, "We will leave that up to you of the younger nature, however, I will need for you to gather me some ground samples."

"Not a problem," Seth answered.

After another cup of coffee, they all went back to their tents to gather their gear for descending into the crater. Airy was standing beside Sonya when Seth approached them.

"Ladies, lead the way and we will get to it," he gave them a quick grin flashing his dimples.

A guard was there to escort them up to the large hole. Seth took some time to scout around the rim of the crater before he was ready to descend. The guard watched as the group anchored off to two very large trees some 10 feet away.

Seth tossed his rope over the edge and started descending, after several minutes, he yelled up, "So far good ground be careful and watch your footing." The women looked at each other then Airy began with Sonya following. Seth gathered one sample for Dr. Semen as he waited for the women to join him. "Well, what do you think so far?"

"Looks like a hole to me, I don't see any cracks or any real jagged edges," Airy commented.

"The dirt should actually be extremely loose and most earthquakes make a much smaller hole more in tune to a fracture, a jagged slice or fissure-like opening. Some indentions can be as wide as 20 to 30 feet or more and 90 feet deep is the average to large voids. The seismic rating for this was minor at 2.4 so when the seismologist came to inspect this since earthquakes are virtually unheard of here; he noticed how large and became confused. He walked the rim and made several measurements and after he made camp, he apparently noticed the light and immediately reported to his superiors that he didn't believe the crater happened through an earthquake and couldn't explain the light that arose. That is when the government became involved. I reviewed the notes and that was about all the information he reported as factual. Moreso, he made several speculations that this may have been a bombed area, however, it lacked the loose dirt that would have been evident with both a bomb and or an earthquake."

"So, if not an earthquake, then what?" Airy questioned.

"We aren't certain that is one of the main reasons we are here. They wanted only specialists in the fields and since the seismologist and his superior were confused and were two of the leading men in their field, the government saw no need to bring them out here again. I was immediately contacted by a government official that I attended university with and he asked me to read the report and decide what others were needed in order to find results."

"So, you are actually in charge?" Airy asked surprised.

"Yes, but Dr. Kellser seems to think he is and that I am his assistant because he is always asking me to do things for him and I politely remind him he is only here because I invited him aboard. You know men around here have a hard time taking orders, or for that matter suggestions from a woman."

"So, I've been told," Airy turned to look at Seth who was listening to the conversation but had seen no reason to chime in.

"Well, everything seems fine let's carry on," Sonya stated.

They moved deeper into the crater and the dirt relaxed and began to make the trek unstable at times. They were three-fourths of the way to the area that the mysterious light showed from and Seth stopped and looked at his watch; they were scaling downward for nearly two hours. This was normal speed when you were unsure of the area and taking samples along the way. "We should take a breath here for a moment it looks as if we will soon be upon the narrowing area and the light is just beyond that."

"The dirt is soft with every step do you think it is safe for all of us to descend at once?" Sonya questioned.

"I've climbed most of my life and I have to say the flow isn't favorable; however, I believe it to be safe. We should all take each step softly before putting our full weight into it." Seth knew he was making the accurate choice to continue the climb.

"I usually scale up mountains not down into craters but I agree with Seth it does seem loose but safe enough if we are careful."

"All right, since I've only done this sort of thing a few times I will allow you to lead. That was one of the reasons I asked for someone with experience in this as well."

Seth grabbed another bottle and retrieved another sample of dirt. They each drank from their canteens and once they were replaced in their backpack, they began downward again.

Each step taken was done with watchful control and the process became tedious and only feet from their destination Seth heard Sonya yell out, "Crap!"

Freezing for a split second he looked up and saw her go to the ground in a heap. "Dr. Ramsey, what's wrong?"

"My ankle, I think I twisted it."

"Hold on," he said scaling up toward her some thirty feet away.

Airy who was only feet from her made it to Sonya before Seth finished talking. "Where is the pain, Sonya?"

"The left side hurts the most," she was holding the injured foot.

"Let me take off your boot and we can assess the damage," Airy gently placed Sonya's booted foot in her hands and turned it so she could access the laces. Once they were untied, Seth appeared beside them. Airy said, "I am going to remove the boot as gently as possible." She placed her hand under the heel and the other on top pulling slowly.

"Ouch," Sonya yelled and took in a sharp breath as the boot released her throbbing ankle.

Seth knelt and placed his hand above Airy's as she removed Sonya's sock. "Let's see what damage has been done. It was evident just as soon as the sock came down, her ankle already turning bluish and the medial malleolus was already swollen and protruding twice as round as normal. "We are going to have to radio up and ask for a stretcher to be lowered. You won't be able to climb out of here." Seth stood and took the walkie out of his bag turning the switch on. "Dr. Lock to the top of the crater, this is an emergency, I say again an emergency. Over."

Static played on the line for a second and then, "Dr. Lock, this is Hector how can we help? Over."

"We have an injury, unable to climb; we need a stretcher lowered. Over."

"We receive; stay on the line for further information. Over."

Five minutes passed as Sonya apologized for stopping their task at such a crucial time. Her apology met with sympathy for her pain from her colleagues.

"Dr. Lock, Dr. Lock, this is Hector, we are lowering the stretcher now. Copy?"

"Yes, we copy. Over." Seth looked up and he could see something coming over the edge of the crater with wheels on the bottom. "Your ride will be here soon, Dr. Ramsey. All we can do now is wait."

A good 35 minutes later, they were strapping Sonya onto the canvas frame for transport. "Ready for a slow lift Hector, we will follow with. Over."

"Slow lift we understand, standby. Over."

The litter started to move slowly and Seth followed on the right as Airy did the same on the left. Now and then, the ground would snag the transport and they would have to shift it so it could continue up the side of the crater. It took a lot longer going up than coming down and nightfall emerged as they reached the rim of the chasm. There was only one medically trained personnel, an officer in the army. He examined Sonya's leg when they were topside. His opinion was that she sustained a bad sprain resulting from a ligament tear most likely, and that she stepped wrong causing the foot inward and the ankle outward, which is why the medial malleolus is affected so badly. He handed her some pain pills and a bottle of water. Then he ordered four men to carry her on the stretcher to her tent. Thus, informing her that there was no ice and a bucket would be brought to her with stream water. For the next two hours, to gingerly placed her foot and ankle in the bucket soaking it. He'd be around to bandage it up later.

Airy went to the buffet with Seth and gathered food for herself and Sonya, she also grabbed two canned sodas and placed them in her pockets along with the eating utensils and sought out Sonya's tent leaving Seth to eat with the others. Pushing the flap open with her elbow she entered saying, "Hello, Sonya, it's Airy I have brought dinner for us."

Sonya smiled as Airy entered her tent, "That's so kind of you, Airy, I was hungry, but no one was around for me to ask for food."

"I didn't think that anyone would have so I took the liberty to help out and I kinda had another motive, since we are the only female personnel here and I feel like we have become quick friends. I hope you don't mind my presumption."

"I also feel like we have become friends in a short time and I also would enjoy becoming better acquaintances with you," Sonya's English accent was present in her words.

"Great," Airy said as she put down both plates on a small table near Sonya's mat which was on the ground. Sonya sat in the only chair in the room with her foot soaking in the stream water. Airy pulled the sodas out of her pockets and handed Sonya one and the utensils and then she grabbed the plate off the table and handed that to her too. She found a spot across from her new friend and sat down on the ground then popped the tab on her soda and took her plate off the table and they both began to eat. A few bites in Airy asked, "How's your ankle feeling?"

"The pain meds have kicked in a little and the throbbing isn't as bad though I don't think the water is helping much."

"Well, I guess being wrapped will help."

"Yes, the compression should keep the swelling down. So, tell me about yourself, Airy."

"Not a lot to tell, I am from Houston, Texas, and gathered my degree at the University of Texas in Austin at the Jackson School of Geosciences. I am an only child and my dad and I climbed together because my mom hated heights; we did lots of things together. I do things with Mom too; we are quite close it's just our relationship is different. I became interested in archeology as a small child because of my grandfather's love of artifacts his profession was an artifact analyst, although he passed away four years ago. I still miss him."

"My grandfather also influenced me to become a geologist because of his passion for rocks of all kinds. He used to collect them and tell me about them. I could sit for hours with him listening to him talk about rocks. He picked them up from everywhere he traveled. He purchased some also and he knew about so many more that he only had pictures of."

As Sonya spoke, Airy realized that her age was only slightly higher than her own maybe by eight years. "What university did you attend?"

"The University of Tasmania, in Australia, I graduated eight years ago and I have done field study ever since, I love being out in nature."

"Then I suppose this isn't your first time with an injury?"

"No, it isn't. Airy, may I ask a personal question."

"Sure," Airy liked Sonya and she felt at ease with her so she wasn't wary of anything the woman would ask.

"Are you and Dr. Lock a thing?"

"What?"

"Are you two you know, dating or anything?"

"No, we just met."

"Oh. Well, I noticed some looks between you two so I thought maybe you were..."

"No."

"So, you have no designs on him."

"No, I mean when we first met, he was arrogant, but now I just think he's a...I guess he's a nice guy, but I don't like, like him or anything."

"Okay, so if I believed him to be sexy, and would like to make a move on him you would be okay with that?"

Airy didn't know why Sonya wanting Seth bothered her, but it did. She thought he was handsome and a little dreamy with his goatee, but she didn't have feelings for him he was a colleague, so why did it bother her?

"Airy."

"Oh, what was it you were saying?"

"I just don't want to step on your toes now that we have become friends. If I am butting in, I understand and will leave him alone, it is just that there are so few men that interest me."

"No, like I said he has only become a friend as you are now."
"Great."

The rest of their conversation was slightly heard. Airy was still trying to figure out why Sonya's attraction to Seth troubled her. Had he come to mean more to her in a few days, was she attracted to him, did she want more than a friendship from him? Could her only interest be someone else possessed designs on him? She questioned herself. It didn't matter now she gave Sonya her consent to pursue him, not that she shouldn't have, he didn't belong to her.

Chapter Five

Two hours into their trek the following day they were nearing the area where their coworker made a detour in their mission.

"Are you ready to finally figure out this mystery? Seth asked Airy with a slightly mischievous voice.

"I've been ready, let's do this," she answered with anticipation bubbling forth.

"Okay, remember safety first."

Airy looked up at Seth with a broad smile on her face realizing that in the next few minutes, they were going to be the first to see and analyze what lay ahead. Answers to the question of the coordinates and the overall mystery were about to be solved. She wanted to jump to the lower area but Seth's words came back haunting her, safety first, the words blaring pausing her footsteps. "Seth, do you think I could peer into the area first? I know that you are in charge and have more experience but I'd like to be the initial one to lay eyes on whatever it is. I want to be the first to gaze at the wonder."

"To be the first to take credit now that you are on an official dig since graduating. This could be a critical stepping stone in your career," he answered a little confrontational.

"No. yes, I mean I am just so excited I just want to see it first."

Thinking back to his first excavation he said, "How about we do this together as a team that way we both share recognition."

"I'd like that very much," she grinned her green eyes beaming under her golden lashes.

Seth sucked in his breath at the sight of her. She was more beautiful than he thought back in the hotel dining room. He scarcely reflected on that night until now because the business at hand acquired his total awareness, however gazing at her now he could think of nothing else. It made his feet heavy as if stuck in the mud, and he couldn't seem to take a step. It made his mind and eyes fuzzy and he blinked several times to clear the fog that covered him.

"Are you coming? I thought we were doing this together?" Airy interrupted his musing.

Taking the leads off to the ropes that helped them down into the crater and switching to the ones that needed to be attached to the steep mountainside to help them propel the wall about fifteen feet to move toward the opening. Airy dragged out the carabiner attachment along with the piton to hammer into the mountainside.

"We should document this; let me retrieve the video recorder I brought." Seth gathered his gear and the hammer then retrieved the camera.

"I was so thrilled I didn't think. I have things to learn if I desire to be lead on any expedition."

Being as cautious as the wall would allow, they moved forward. Slowly and with focus, they entered the area of importance, both with their expectations of the find and Seth's documentation to certify the discovery. They observed a hole in the side of the mountain and as they approached, trepidation crept into their bodies. Looking at each other with a puzzled gaze, neither spoke. Only more questions that at this point they couldn't seem to voice. A puncture plain and simple. The outside of the opening was round and a little disturbance of dirt and grass was seen. They both wondered if this was the spot, or if the light was somewhere else beyond them because the hole was minuscule less than the size of a cantaloupe. From the light above at night it looked expansive. It was daylight now so they knew that the light wouldn't be easily perceived, though something should shine. Why was there nothing?

Seth reached for his bag, "Airy, hold the camera let me take a closer look." He fished out a flashlight and peered into the cavity outlet seeing no light, no reflection, no quarts-type rock, only blackness.

"What is it, Seth?" she questioned with impatience.

"Take a look for yourself," he took the camera back and handed her the flashlight.

She looked deep inside and after a minute she said, "There's not anything, just space."

"That's what I noticed too," he didn't like seeing the disappointment written across her face.

"How can that be? Do we have the right spot?"

"It should be here."

"Well, nothing is here, we must look around, it has to be nearby, we must have the wrong location."

Seth felt certain it was the correct area though it was practical to look farther. Placing the video recorder back in his pack he helped Airy look beyond the mountain opening. They were dangling on ropes moving slowly along searching for some other type of cavity or any source of light. Farther from the opening than anything should be and yet nothing even gave pause to the anomaly. "Airy, we have moved significantly away from the projected spot. We should stop."

"But it must be here we are just overlooking the site."

"Airy, I know how disappointed you are, we just need to gather our thoughts and maybe even revise the observed angles. You know accurate measurements were impossible from far away and above."

She left her shoulders as well as her hopes slump; it wasn't what she expected when she opened her eyes this morning. Her expectation crushed making her feel physically ill.

Seth caught up to her and placed his warm hand on her shoulder trying to give her the comfort and encouragement he knew she needed.

Glancing up into his brown sympathetic eyes, she half smiled, "I imagine I need to be tougher if I expect to get any respect in this field?"

"I won't say anything if you don't," he gave a little grin of his own.

"Okay let's look at what we know so far. The distance originally calculated was 880 meters which is over half a mile correct?"

"Yes, but we didn't do the computation, we took what was already done before we arrived. So, we need to go back and see how they arrived with that number," he answered.

"We gazed at the lights the past two nights and without doing any calculations of my own I would have said it was down about a half mile."

"And that is just what I am referring to, the light cannot be judged by appearances because of its refractive properties, the angle, the size, or even its intensity. I should have done my own computations before we made the trek down into this crater."

She could hear the frustration in his voice, but she would have never dreamt of reassessing the statistics of another scientist, to do so would seem egotistical. "Do you feel the calculations are incorrect?"

"I don't know but there is a chance."

"So, we go all the way up the crater just to return tomorrow? That seems like a waste to me."

"Yes, I also feel like it is a misuse of time and effort; however, there is nothing more we can do from here. Agreed?"

"I hate to give in so easily, although like you I don't see another solution." Her mind was turning trying to find another way but like Seth, she could find nothing that would suffice. Looking up at Seth again and then at the top of the crater, hating what they needed to do she said, "Wait, I need to know we have done everything possible. Let's look around a little more, please. We have plenty of time before it's necessary to return and still have time to run more figures once we are topside."

"Airy, I understand how much this means to you but our time is important and I don't want to delay it needlessly."

"But...."

Seth cut her off before she could say more. "Let's go." He hated being brass with her but this was the most rational course.

Airy heard the annoyance in his voice when he interrupted her and she knew he felt she was acting like an inexperienced student. It wounded her to know he viewed her that way, even for a moment, though he was right that was the most logical decision but she couldn't help herself, giving up hope wasn't something she was accustomed to.

As they climbed, Airy told herself that she wasn't giving up the situation required more time and facts and they would return tomorrow and see what destiny had in store. She planted one foot after the other until they were at the top edge of the crate. They made it in record time now that they were surer of their footing on the soft ground. The hour-long trek was in mostly silence due to both parties being deep in thought.

. . ⚜ . .

"AIRY, MAY I COME IN?"

"Yes," she answered just putting away the clothes she used down in the depression today. When Seth entered, she felt relief that she changed and looked presentable to him with her hair loosely lying over the shoulder of her purple tank top.

She smelled of rose water and his nostrils couldn't help drinking in the scent of her. He noticed she cleaned up and changed and he wished at that moment he did also; though he was busy taking measurements, and all for nothing. "Airy, I hope this isn't an interruption; however, I wanted to tell you that the calculations given to us were accurate, at least as far as I can tell. This isn't my field of expertise but we should have been on top of the site."

"I don't understand. Why wasn't it there?"

"I think we did find it and for some reason just didn't see the anomaly. I talked with Sonya, Dr. Kellser, and Dr. Semen about the light and whether they composed their own calculations on its position. Dr. Kellser said he did when he first arrived and his were the same as mine. As you know, I needed to wait until dark to finish and by all accounts, we are correct."

"So, what do we do now?"

"Well, I believe we have a solution," he smiled, his dimples raised.

"Don't keep me in suspense what is it?"

It took him a second to recover as her smile, brighter than any sun, beamed her enthusiasm across the room to him. "Kellser believes the light that shines may need a little help being seen by the naked eye in the daylight because it's an infrared light and he suggests we use night vision goggles and Sonya agreed."

"That sounds great in theory, but where are we supposed to get night vision goggles? It's not like the army surplus store is right down the road," her smile fading away at the lack of a solution to their problem.

"No, but we have army guards all around us."

Airy's smile flashed again and she leaped at Seth hugging his neck and squeezing him tightly in excitement. After, a few moments embarrassment set in and she retreated regretting her actions.

Seth took a step backward as well before speaking, "I will talk with the guards and gather what we need and see you in the morning." He turned and exited the tent as fast as he could. As he made, his way to the guards he wondered why he retreated so quickly when all he wanted to do was kiss her soft pale lips.

· · ◈ · ·

WHEN MORNING ARRIVED, Airy was up with the sun and as she eagerly peeked outside the flap of her tent, she felt elated to see the hustle and bustle of camp. Like herself, it seemed as if everyone impatiently wanted to see what the crater contained. The news that they may have answers today made the anticipation in the crew and soldiers intensify. A grin spread across her face as she walked toward Sonya's tent. "Knock, Knock, are you in Sonya, it's Airy."

"Yes, come in, Airy."

She pulled open the flap and walked in talking as she did, "I came to see how your ankle is feeling and if you need breakfa...." Shocked to see Seth inside she didn't complete her question.

Sonya looked at Airy with a large grin and said, "Thank you for thinking about me, I am good. Seth and I just finished eating, and look he made me a crutch," she said with enthusiasm.

"That's great," Airy answered after finding her voice, but she had a strange feeling there was more to him being in Sonya's tent.

"We will be leaving soon; did you eat yet?" Seth questioned.

She thought it odd that he seemed capable of speaking and she found it hard to get herself to think let alone talk.

"Airy, is something wrong? You look flushed?" Sonya asked.

"No, she answered still finding it hard to say anything. Looking around the tent, she noticed Sonya's bed in disarray, her hair was loosely flowing over her face, and it suddenly hit her that she walked in on a tryst between lovers. Her face reddened more and she quickly backed out of the tent saying, "I'm going to go get some food before it is gone. See you in a little while." Almost running she proceeded toward her tent and slammed into the man called Dex.

Grabbing Airy's shoulders he pushed her back and said, "What's the hurry, Honey." His eyes gleamed with a cold black glare.

Airy felt frightened, she'd been warned not to look into the eyes of the men from this country, to stay away from them, to keep to herself, and to refrain from speaking to them as much as possible. But as she stood frozen like a deer in headlights, her mind could think of nothing to say to excuse herself and get away. She moved to go around his large frame.

Dex placed his arm out in front of her stopping Airy. "You need to apologize for your rudeness," he said coldheartedly.

Airy tried not to look at him and spoke more to the air than to him, "I'm very sorry for the disrespect, and I apologize for bumping into you." The words stuck in her throat and her stomach. She hated bowing down just because he was a man. She tried to leave again and again his arm rose stopping her.

"I think I should make you earn my forgiveness."

His voice was menacing as he spoke. Airy stood her ground she had enough of this. Her apology was met with scorn. She only knew one other way; the way Americans do things when politeness doesn't work. She looked up at the big man who tried his hardest to intimidate her, straightened her spine, and deepened her voice. Speaking with authority she said, "Get out of my way, I have apologized, and if that isn't good enough then too bad, now let me pass."

"Where do you think you are? No one speaks to me......"

"Can I be some assistance?" Seth came up behind Airy and placed a belonging hand on the small of her back.

Dex's arm fell toward the ground and he cleared his throat. "No, the little lady was just leaving," his voice rough as he spoke.

"Fine, fine." Seth pushed on Airy's back herding her away. He'd seen from across camp how rigid she was and the callous look on Dex's face and knew he needed to run interference before something went terribly wrong. Directing Airy toward a nearby tree, he removed his hand from the small of her back and asked, "What do you think you were doing antagonizing him?"

She fumed and clamped her mouth closed before she told him how she didn't need his interference when she was putting that brute in his place, and now he may never respect her and think she is someone who has to have a man for protection. Daggers shot from her eyes, she wanted to scream profanity at him, but wouldn't cause a scene in front of the people looking on. "Everything was under control," she finally said angrily.

He noticed the tight edge in her voice and wondered why it felt like she directed irritation at him. "I was hoping to gather our gear and leave for the crater soon."

"We can go now, I am ready."

"I thought you were going to get breakfast?"

"I'm not hungry. Let's go." Airy turned and started toward the shed-like building where their gear was now stored.

Seth followed, wondering what transpired between Airy and Dex, and why she seemed to be taking out her aggression on him.

．． ⚓ ．．

THE HIKE DOWN INTO the crater was made at a faster pace. They both knew where to go and the stability of the ground. After reaching their destination both breathed a sigh of relief with the ease of the descent. Airy removed the baseball cap that Seth gave her the other day, to ward off the sun. She wiped the sweat now dripping into her eyes with the blue bandanna she wore around her neck.

"It is much hotter today, here." Seth handed Airy a metal water bottle.

"Thanks," she replied begrudgingly not yet over the episode of this morning.

They hooked the other rope on made sure it was secure and descended the fifteen feet. "Okay, now that we have arrived, we need the goggles. He began to dig the glasses out of his backpack; retrieving them he handed the infrared readers to Airy, and asked, "Would you like to do the honors?"

"Yeah," she answered, hostility lingering. She placed the goggles in front of her eyes and felt a surge of enthusiasm reaching out before her, "I can see the light it is right in front of me." Her hand tried to find the opening.

Seth slid beside her and directed her hand toward the cavity and a slight electrical shot went through them both. Seth pulled back as did Airy.

"What was that?" she asked.

"Nothing, just static." Seth wasn't sure why almost every time he touched her skin that static electricity passed through him, but at least she experienced it this time too, so he knew it wasn't just his imagination.

Airy placed the glasses to her eyes again and looked in the hole, the lights were bright as they beamed toward her, and difficult to look at for more than a few seconds. "Here you look," she handed the goggles to Seth enthusiastically.

He placed them in front of his eyes holding them a few inches away and looked into the cavity. The lights danced before him with brilliant colors, but he couldn't tell what was making the dazzling show and why it would shine like a beacon at night.

"So, what do you think?" Airy asked impatiently.

"You tell me?" He couldn't help the smile that spread across his face as he took in Airy's excitement and it made him realize he was starting to have real feelings for her.

"I don't know. Aren't you the lead on this don't you have some kind of theory?"

"At this point, we know as much as we did before which is not much." Seth pondered for a moment and seemed to consider something.

Airy caught the gleam in his dark eyes and said, "You are thinking we have to dig, aren't you?"

"You got it. I just so happen to have brought our gear for a little excavation."

"I have my small tools but I wasn't planning on going deep."

"You remember I said once to always be prepared."

"Yep teacher," she smiled.

They were both perspiring as they dangled from their ropes with collapsible shovels, which were comprised of a pick on the opposite end, in their hands. The sun was signaling late afternoon and they both knew if they didn't reach it today then they would need to come back tomorrow.

First, Airy then Seth wiped at the sweat on their faces. Airy pulled on Seth's backpack and he naturally turned so she could get the water bottle out. They'd been going at this for hours so they were like a well-oiled machine, dig, sweat, wipe, drink. She handed him the bottle he took a big sip and handed it back. Airy placed it in the pack and looked back at the opening they created. It was large but not very deep within. As archeologists and paleontologists, they knew whatever they did that protecting the find was the most important obstacle and that meant they needed to go slow and careful even using larger tools; because along the way they may damage something that they didn't know existed.

Time was running out for the day and Seth looked up at the now-sunless sky and then at his watch it read quarter till five, and in West Africa, the sun usually set near six-thirty this time of year so this was cutting it close. They would need to start up so they wouldn't be trying to climb in the darkness. Seth placed his hand on Airy's arm, "We need to stop for today."

"No, just a little mor..." She felt deflated, they were so close, she sensed it.

"Airy, I said time to stop, you need to stop thinking you are in charge." Reaching into his pack to replace his tools he heard Airy shriek in joy.

"I have it. I feel it, Seth. I can touch it."

It's hard like a rock, no something softer." She stretched her fingers pushing her shoulder into the dirt and rock wall reaching for the light source within, and then she cried out as the item sent a shock unlike, she'd ever experienced through her fingers to her body and everything went silent and dark as she shot backward through the air.

Chapter Six

"Have the doctors told you any else?" A frantic woman asked Seth when he stood up and introduced himself.

"No, Mrs. Sheppard, he said at three today he should know more. He is waiting for some scan results to come back. I am so sorry that this happened."

"Yes, you were very vague when you called as to what specifically took place." Airy's father questioned the young man before him.

"Yes, Sir, I know it seems that way but there is very little that I can tell you because it happened so quickly. The only other thing I can say is this was an excavation that was set up by the African government and we were protected while here by the military as well as guards I hired. There were no other indications that something this tragic could happen."

"Stop it, John. We are here to be with Airy not interrogated. She told us before she left that this dig was a dream come true and no one could stop her from going, and you know accidents happen and things sometimes go wrong."

"You're right, Maryann, it just sounds strange that a person could put their hand in a hole where there is a light and go into a coma."

"I understand, I was there and it happened to be the strangest thing I have ever witnessed. One second, she was talking to me and the next she jerked backward and fell limp. You must understand that we were down in the dig site when this happened, two hours from the top of the crater. I radioed up but it took us nearly three hours to get her to the top and then we didn't get her life-flighted out for four more due to our remote location."

"Can we discuss this later I want to sit with my daughter?"

"Yes, Ma'am. Please excuse me I will be in the waiting room if you need anything more from me." Seth walked out and down the hall to the waiting area where he spent too much time in the past few days. First awaiting word of Airy's condition and afterward waiting for any change. He was either in her room by the bed talking to her or making calls, but sometimes for a change of scenery, he'd go to the waiting area.

.. ⚓ ..

NEARLY TWO WEEKS WITH no change in Airy's condition. The coma they were told could last for weeks or she may never regain consciousness. They couldn't find any reason for her state but did notice on the scans that brain activity in the left hemisphere was heightened as if she was in REM sleep. This wasn't truly abnormal in itself, however, the activity they discovered is much more than others in a coma-like state.

Seth spent most of his time at the hospital with Airy's unconscious body and her parents. They shared stories of her childhood through her college time and he felt as if he now knew her on a personal level. A familiarity, with her personality and her likes and dislikes. He grasped a sense of who she was and why, and he liked the person he was told about, but of course, he would, because he liked her when he barely knew anything about her. He held a vigil at her bedside, talking to her and even telling her about himself. Seth talked about, life lessons, his fears, and how he'd grown fond of her before the accident occurred. He'd begged her to fight and wake up to end his tortured fate.

Seth never returned to the dig site since Airy's accident. The region was roped off completely awaiting the military and government officials' report that gave the all-clear to continue work. When it was finally given added precautions were put in place: more medical personnel and equipment along with additional excavation tools and another geologist since Sonya was injured also.

Seth's uncle arrived in Monrovia the prior day, in time for the lift to the all-stop order to be given on the site. Seth would be required to return and continue the dig. He despised leaving Airy and her parents since he felt responsible for what happened, his leadership brought about her injuries, and she may never regain consciousness again, and may even die because of him.

Yesterday when he met up with Stephen they went directly to the hospital, and after visiting Airy they talked about why it was necessary that they find answers to the mystery and how that served to help them figure out what happened to Airy, in that hole. Why she's now in a coma and if something they discovered might bring her out of it?

The officials of Western Africa wanted to meet before Seth and Stephen departed for Mt. Nimba. They waited at the hotel restaurant for the head of West Africa's political affairs officer. He had been placed in charge due to the area of the sphere and because he wasn't military, he protected the health and welfare of the country.

A group of men entered the restaurant and were directed toward their table, the official introduced himself and took a seat, while the others in his group waited by the door. "Gentlemen, thank you for meeting with me and let me tell you how sorry we were to hear of your colleague's accident. Has there been any change in her condition?"

"Thank you but no change," Seth said sadly.

"Again sorry, though we must continue with the business at hand. I have read all the reports and visited the site yesterday and I need to inform you that we are being pressured to complete this job. Gentlemen, the military will be formally taking over this project in a few weeks if you cannot provide us with more information by that time."

The group spoke again of what the object could be and what it did with just one touch. Neither man could make heads or tails of why a glowing rock-like object would harm someone, why it was embedded in the side of a mountain, and why it caused seismic activity.

"Sir, you must understand that at a dig site, it could take months to unearth an object so it isn't damaged," Morard explained.

"Yes, I know this but we have come to the point that time is essential. Try your best not to damage it however we need it out now, do what you must because I am afraid once our military hands begin extracting the object it will be done swiftly without care and they will be the ones then doing any testing or examination of the find with their scientist, and you know they will only be looking for ways it can help the military."

"Yes Sir, we understand."

Standing he said one last thing. "Our going it before the military is crucial so I hope for all our sakes you will make this happen."

. . ⚜ . .

STEPHEN TOSSED HIS case in the back of the jeep and climbed inside sitting next to his nephew. "I am very excited, Seth this could be a landmark discovery."

"Yes, that is possible but at this point I just need answers."

"We shall attempt to find them my boy, and I, like you, hope it will be useful in helping Mrs. Sheppard. Airy through the years was not only one of the brightest students that I taught; her enthusiasm for our discipline was contagious. I do wish she was coming along, but we shall go forward in hopes of aiding her. You will be going back into the crater for the first time since the accident and I want you to stay in contact at all times and be very careful. Your parents would never forgive me if something happened to you."

"I hold myself responsible for what happened with Airy, though I wasn't the lead on the entire project, I was the lead in charge of her."

"I know, my boy, and I would like to tell you not to however if I were in your shoes, I also would hold myself responsible, even though no one could predict such a thing. I see no fault on you for what happened."

"My brain tells me you are right but, my heart says I should have gone over every procedure and explained why we must follow rules. If I had then maybe she wouldn't be in that bed and lifeless." Seth's head bent forward as he punished himself.

"Seth, is there more to this?"

"What do you mean?"

"I don't know it seems that you are making more than is obligatory out of an accident."

"I've never had someone get injured who worked under my management."

"Like I said this wasn't something that could be controlled. If you know Airy as I do then you know she is impulsive, curious, and though intelligent she was most likely overwhelmed, eager and just didn't think, you didn't need to tell her not to touch the unknown."

"Yes, but I wasn't thinking either. I should have directed her to remove her hand right away but I didn't and now she may die."

"Then let's make sure it wasn't for nothing. We find out what it is and why this happened and we do so in her name, agreed?"

Seth mumbled yes and began to revise his plan to gain access to what was in the crater.

• • ⚜ • •

"I FEEL WE ARE ON THE precipice of an exciting discovery however caution must be at the forefront of everything you do from here on," Morard explained to all gathered.

Seth threw his rope over the edge and into the chasm as did his new partner, Zackary Patton, whom Sonya Ramsey contacted to take her position on the dig. She was on-site nonetheless her leg up to her knee now in a cast brace awaiting surgery on her ankle.

Zackary graduated from Tasmania University in Australia, with Sonya. He was born and raised in Sydney; his accent was thickly Aussy.

At times Seth had trouble understanding his new associate as they descended into the crater.

It didn't take long for them to become at ease with each other being alike in a lot of areas of their lives. They arrived at the intended point quickly taking less than the normal time, and took off the lead ropes that helped them into the crater. They attached ropes that were stronger and shorter to hold their weight so they could move to the opening; these ropes would fasten them to the mountainside.

"So, as I stated earlier, we are going to dig a circular area around this light source and extract it intact with soil around it and try to place it in this foldable box I got from the military. Keeping safety in mind, we proceed with these electrical gloves I brought down so we don't touch the article directly. Our only problem from what I know now is we don't have a discerning dimension on the object so I am hoping it will fit inside this chest." Seth stated as he took the plastic four sides item out of the bag, he had been dragging down the mountain crater with him. It was black with plastic walls and a lid. He took a rope tied it on, and then attached that rope to his lead. Then he looked at Zackary and said, "Ready to go get this thing?"

"All righty, Mate," Zack answered excitedly.

The two slid down the steep slope of the mountainous rock area. Both men looking for a quick end to what they were to do but that would not be something that either would achieve. The work was slow as they began encountering larger rocks once they passed through the soil's top layer. By late afternoon, they concluded that the tools were not going to be sufficient for the scope of this project. A return to base camp and new tools would start tomorrow's job anew.

. . ⚜ . .

"CRIKKIE IT IS HOT. This thing is really solid inside this mountain."

Seth wanted to say no joke, just keep working you aren't the only one who feels the heat and stress. He held his tongue and nodded.

"Blamhee, have a look at this another pick broke and I am on my third hammer, Mate. Blasted heat," Zack wiped his brow.

"What do you want me to do?" Seth couldn't hold back any longer. Zachary had been complaining the past three days about tools, work, heat, and food and he couldn't take another word from his mouth, sometimes things went slow, and if he was, a paleontologist he'd know patients was the name of the game.

"Mate, I know you are used to this tedious work but there has to be another way. Whatasay we dynamite this thing, ain't gonna come out any other way."

"I am open to reasonable suggestions. I have used everything I can think of that will leave this thing undamaged; all I can say is that we just have to keep going."

"Say we do and finally get past the object just how far back do we go into this bloody mountainside? At this rate, it may take years."

He wasn't wrong and Seth considered that saying nothing. Maybe, it was time to call it or gather outside opinions as to how to gain access, and as he was considering just that when Zack said, "Hey, I got a mate that works in the oil field they have to go through rock all the time, let me give him a call and see if he can tell me anything that will work. It's a three-day trip back you think they will let us stop for that long?"

"The government has been informed of our problems; I think with a possible solution they will agree. Besides a helicopter is due in the morning with new provisions so I bet we can hitch a ride and be there in a few hours. But I caution you to not tell him where we are working or what we are trying to extract out of the mountainside."

"I could use a pint, Mate, after the past few days we've had. What'we waiting for Mate? You gather the rest of the tools," he said as he placed a hammer, pick, and small shovel in his pack and went to relieve himself.

Seth was getting better at deciphering his companions' long-drawn-out words and strange terms and he wondered why their English accent in Australia was nothing like their mother country.

· · ~~ · ·

"YEAH, THAT'S RIGHT Cal," Zack was saying into his phone after tagging up with his friend. "What is the name of that machine again? A Speed Diamond Core Driller and you want me to take off the stand and add pipe that will extend the length, and what about the water it needs?"

The voice on the other end of the line said, "Gather a couple of five-gallon lightweight canisters to carry on your backs. That should get you through about 4 hours each. Make sure you stop now and then to let the machine rest."

"Thanks, Cal for the help," he hung up the phone and looked over at Seth, "Here is a list of what we need."

Seth pulled out his wallet and handed Zack a visa card, can you manage to get everything I'd like to go to the hospital and check on Airy."

"Mate, you went this morning. I bet her condition is the same. You need to stop brooding." Zack was worried about his new colleague he hadn't been much for conversation since they left the site. His mind was elsewhere and he knew it was because Seth felt responsible for the accident and told him as much.

"I know but we may be up on that refugee for a while so I want to see for myself one last time before we leave tomorrow. I will call the helicopter service; the government said we could get them to take us back up."

"Okay, Mate."

"Let me know if you have any problems."

"Will do."

Seth went to the hospital. Airy's father was outside sitting on a bench right off of the parking area, his head bent low. Seth wondered if something happened and he almost didn't want to disturb him to find out. He didn't want to know if Airy was gone, his mind wandered towards her constantly as he worked, sometimes to the point of distraction. With his head low on his shoulders, he placed a hand on Mr. Sheppard's upper back.

The older man raised his head, "Oh, hey, Seth. Are you leaving or coming?"

"Coming, Sir. Is everything all right," his voice dipped low with a slight quiver.

"The same I'm afraid. The doctor came in and told us they wanted to send her to a long-term care facility. They wanted us to prepare for that last week but we told them no, now I think it may be best. We refuse to have them take her off the breathing tube, so that is our only other option."

"I see."

"Her mother cries every day and I don't know how much longer I can be strong for them both. The doctors still don't know why she won't wake up. Her brain is functioning as well as her heart, and organs, and the only reason they placed a breathing tube in was because her breathing stayed extremely shallow."

"I ....."

Maryann Sheppard ran through the hospital doors screaming and waving her arms in the air, "John, John she's awake! Our girl is awake!" Breathless Maryann now stood in front of her husband, "She just woke up, and she knows me."

John Sheppard stood with all the grief he was feeling earlier now erased from his face. "Is she okay?"

"I don't know but she did smile at me before the doctor asked me to leave while he removed the breathing tube. I knew I had to find you."

"Well, what are we waiting for folks let's go," Seth spoke up alleviated.

·· ⚜ ··

THAT EVENING SETH AND Zack were in a pancake house down the road from the hotel. "How're your eggs and pancakes, Mate?"

"What?" Seth's thoughts were heavy since Airy awoke, he'd been by her bedside every second; and since he stayed there, her parents were using the opportunity to catch up on vital sleep knowing that their daughter was well and in good company.

Airy conveyed a fantastic story to him of amazing feats and unknown history. She told him she had seen things in her mind that even she was unable to understand but she knew it was real. He and her parents tried to tell her she had been dreaming while in a coma, and that is the only reasonable explanation for what she felt was factual, however, her determination remained.

Seth didn't tell Zack or even his uncle when he talked to him over the radio. He didn't want anyone to think her insane; the things she said seemed implausible. He only hoped that she would calm down and stop saying such insane things in front of the doctors and nurses. A psychologist came in yesterday to meet with her and he told them that she was just having trouble deciphering her dreams from reality. This was common for people who have been unconscious for a long period.

"I was just asking about the food you are pushing around on your plate, Mate?"

"Zack, have you experienced a dream or a feeling and felt like it really happened?"

"Yeah, probably for a second or two. Why?"

"Nothing, guess I was just.... Nothing."

"Well, if you ask me nothing got you deep in thought."

"Yeah, maybe a little. Have you heard anything on the ETA on the parts you ordered?"

"The man at the East End Duce Drilling said he'd call as soon as they arrive, it should be before three tomorrow though."

"Good, we need to get back. I'm going to go see Airy and her family."

"Sure, glad she is okay."

Seth pushed out his chair and stood to leave, he ran his hand through his dark thick hair, he couldn't stop thinking about what Airy told him about people in the past. People, called the Kabyars developed on Earth 200 million years ago. Shaking his head again, he wished this wasn't happening to her.

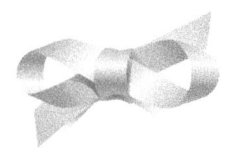

Chapter Seven

Airy was sitting up in bed when Seth walked in. She noticed the concerned look written across his brow and wondered if what she told him yesterday had him feeling apprehensive. She knew it was a lot to take in and if she hadn't experienced it directly, she would have believed it.

"How are you feeling today? I see you ate some breakfast," he attempted to lighten the distress he felt.

Glancing at the hospital tray on the table beside her she said, "They left it here hoping I would eat more, though my appetite hasn't returned my throat is sensitive."

"I'm sure they realize that."

"Seth, I want to thank you for sitting with me while I was.... you know out of it. My parents said you were here most of the time right after."

"They told you about the time I spent here?"

"Yes, but I knew."

"What?"

"I heard you a few times when my mind was not as connected to the Kabyars."

"So, you still think what you were dreaming about is real?"

"I know it was, Seth."

"The doctors said...."

"I don't give a damn what they believe. It was real." Airy paused for a moment calming herself and pleaded, "Will you hear me out before you discount what I know is true?"

"I owe you that much."

"Before I start, I want to thank you again for caring for me after ... it was very kind of you."

"Airy, I would like to tell you something before you begin if that's okay?"

"Go ahead."

"I felt so guilty about what happened."

"You shouldn't."

"That's what everyone says, but I did and still do. At first, I believed it was because I neglected to take certain precautions to keep you safe, but later once I returned to that crater where that light nearly zapped you to death. I realized it was because before all this happened I.... I well; I began to have feelings for you. My guilt was out of emotional concern that someone that had become important to me may die." He took her hand in his, ignoring the static charge that went between them, and caressed the back of it with his thumb, the warmth claiming them both. How could he tell her she now meant more to him than his own life? That he had fallen in love with her even as she lay unconscious.

"You had feelings for me, but I thought you and Sonya were...were well.... lovers."

"What?"

"You were in her tent that morning and well, Sonya told me she liked you... and you both looked disheveled."

"Disheveled you say, well that might have been because I didn't sleep very well that night and was eager about getting those night vision goggles and what that meant for the dig. We were to be the first to discover whatever we were about to unearth. If I am being completely truthful, I spent most of the night thinking about you, replaying that hug you gave me, and wishing I'd kissed you and not run out of your tent like a schoolboy afraid of my feelings. I think the feelings I developed scared the hell out of me. Something I never told you is I was married before, years ago. We didn't part on the best of terms. She had been seeing another man at the beginning of our relationship, she ended it after I proposed, but it didn't stay that way. I found out she was cheating and filed for divorce. Quit my field of study and never looked at a woman in the same way again. Not until that night in your tent, maybe in at the hotel."

She couldn't believe he was saying he liked her, because, until that moment in the tent, she didn't realize how fond of him she had become. "I shouldn't have assumed you and Soyna had been together. I do tend to leap before I look."

"I want you to know that my feelings were surfacing to the point of distraction. Your parents arrived and told me stories about your life, and I felt even closer to you, but it wasn't until I relived what happened up at the summit that I knew I needed you. I want you to know, to understand how much I care for you before I say; Airy, you must understand how unbelievable people living on earth 200 million years ago, with dinosaurs no less, is going to sound to others."

She shook her head, and then said, "You said you would listen so please take a seat before you write me off as a crazy woman you once liked."

Seth gave in a pulled the chair from under the window to the side of Airy's hospital bed. The room boasts warm lights from the ceiling and pale blue, purple, and white plaid wallpaper behind the bed. For a hospital room, it was a cheery scene though cheerful wasn't what he was feeling.

"Thank you. The Kabyars explained that their culture began much as scientist believes we have, like a primordial soup of just the right ingredients 200 million years ago about forty after the dinosaurs developed. The continent shift had begun, and yes, they lived in the era alongside the dinosaurs. They were initially like cavemen at one time also. They didn't technically become functional like we are today until about 170 million years after they developed. It took another million years before their civilization went far beyond what we could even dream of, and less than 50,000 thousand after that they began searching outside of this world eventually making colonies in other areas of space.

They showed me talking in not words but through what I can only describe as thoughts and pictures in my dream-like state. The Kabyars illustrated their complete lifetime. The atmosphere was very different, their lungs were used to less oxygen. Their bodies were not the same as us, it's hard to describe but they were much larger, their heads more cone-like, and their skin was a blueish color. They lived much longer than we do today. Their mental capacity is so much more advanced than we could ever dream. They used the energy of the earth and sun, which was their power grid. By the time Homo sapiens emerged about 350,000 thousand years ago, they were all in space for more than a couple of million years and they did find a new home, a planet they call Sidko. It was the first but they have scattered throughout the galaxy after the mass exit.

They realized that within our DNA code exists remnants of theirs. They returned from time to time to check on what they called their children and imparted some of their ancient technology to different groups of people developing here. Each visit they left something whether it is technology or a building, such as the pyramids. They do this to help us and to let us know we are not alone. However, it wasn't long after they taught us how to build colossal monuments, to map the stars that they realized the people now on the Earth were very combative and numerous. Our mental capacity did not think of advancement but more of advantages. We started demanding more and more technology, mostly for war, but their technology was something we couldn't possibly be prepared to mentally comprehend. We fought amongst ourselves and boldly attacked them. This was something they feared for our people so staying on the planet or having further interaction soon became impossible. They never considered that their teachings would be forgotten or themselves; but quickly knew it was better for the people of the earth if they didn't remember the Kabyar.

They still visited but tried not to interact with us. They hoped one day they would be able to reveal themselves though knew it would only happen when we were advanced enough to manage the information that they could pass on. That time is now, being brought on. That is why they shot the... station, for lack of a better word. It imparts information, mostly knowledge of them. It activates only with people who have the correct gene in their DNA. You see I was meant to touch it, to be given this information for mankind so we can move forward because something is coming that will destroy the planet."

Seth didn't know how to react, it all seemed unbelievable. A station that held knowledge being shot from somewhere or something beyond the earth from what, people that once lived here, in essence, our ancestors. Looking at Airy, he knew she believed every word she spoke.

"You still think I'm a fruitcake!" she spewed enraged.

"I...."

"How do I convince you."

Just then, Airy's parents entered the room. "Good morning, Airy, how are you feeling today and Seth how are you?" Her father beaming his happiness that his only child was out of the coma, though the two didn't notice the steely look Airy gave Seth.

The group engaged in polite conversation until a Catholic priest came into the room and introduced himself and his companion the bishop of this sector of Africa. This made Seth nervous though no one else seemed bothered by the unexpected arrival of both men. However, if Seth possessed Spiderman's tingling sense of impending danger, then it would be going off with the magnitude of a point 10 on the earthquake scale with the new arrivals. The hospital's priest asked the group after a few minutes if he and the bishop could have a few moments alone with Miss Sheppard and that was the second Seth realized she had told the priest about her dreams while in the coma. What that if true would mean to the religious world was no less than annihilation. Starting with if God did not create Adam and Eve then there was no God. He must stop this before either they commit Airy to a loony bin or she gets herself killed by moral religious citizens.

"Gentlemen, I am afraid the young woman has been through a lot since going into a coma. I hope you understand that at this moment, she needs rest and her family's support." He went over to the priest and bishop and began to usher them out of the room. They tried to convince Seth that they only needed a minute with Miss Sheppard, and only wanted to pray for her healing. Their words were heard but not heeded by Seth as he closed the door behind them.

"What did you do that for? Are you trying to run my life?" Airy shrieked.

"Shhh," he stood in front of the door his hand on the knob listening to the religious leader talk and when they look back at him guarding the area the men huffed and walked down the hall.

"Seth, what is going on?" Maryann questioned, astonished at the young man up until this point she thought of as kind and respectful.

"I am sorry but I couldn't in good conscious let them alone to question your daughter."

"He thinks I've lost my mind."

Both parents looked at Seth and then their daughter.

"No. I don't think you are crazy and no I find everything you told me extraordinary, but...."

"But you don't have faith in me. I wish I could prove it. You said you felt like you knew me and if that were true you would know I would never make up something that could change the world."

"I do know that Airy, but you also just woke up from a coma where the doctors told us you experienced dreams."

"It wasn't a dream, damn it!" she screamed with indignation.

"Ok, say I concede that it wasn't a dream. Tell me what do you think the religious world is going to say? Think about it. God and Jesus are now dead to all! People once lived on earth many millions of years ago. Our DNA holds remnants of theirs so in essence they are our relatives. Everything we thought, we believed was not true. Was never true. What is going to happen to religion once you kill God for all? What do you think people will do?"

Airy looked at him incredulously and then she looked at her parents who looked at her distressingly. "But I can't keep this to myself it means so much to mankind to know the truth about our origins, about so many puzzles of the past. It's my responsibility as a person as an archeologist. I have to....."

Her parents were watching her grappling with what this inevitably meant to mankind and how telling this news would rock the world to its very core.

Realizing she'd already told the priest yesterday; he knew what she knew and he even more than she'd told Seth about them coming soon.

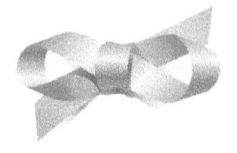

Chapter Eight

Seth explained what needed to be done and how the priest and bishop must view Airy's dreams. He told her parents for now they were to return to Texas and not repeat any of Airy's dreams. If asked say she had nightmares and she wanted to get away for a while and hasn't been in touch.

Seth swept Airy out of the hospital hoping no one would notice her disappearance until it was too late. Though he hadn't expected Airy to fight him on his plan, her strong will just made her dig her heels in trying to figure out a way that wouldn't damage the world.

"I don't understand why we must hide. I'd rather go back to the dig."

"Airy, I have explained that not just the priest may want the information you believe you have. The parties interested may feel that this is very detrimental to the world and harm you whether true or not so it won't leak out. On the other side, many may want this information told so they can manipulate the outcome and the effects it could have on the world."

Finally, with more persuasion Airy agreed to vanish for a time. Bouncing around from city to city until they made their way out of Africa on a freighter bound for Australia.

. . ⚜ . .

"THESE ARE TO BE MY quarters?" she questioned incredulously once on the freighter.

"Sorry, but this is a merchant ship, not a cruise ship. They were nice enough to give you this closet as a room so you don't have to share with the workers."

"But there is only a small bed."

"I'll bunk with the men; you have it all to yourself."

"No, Seth, I...I don't want to be left alone," how could she tell him it wasn't so much being alone as longing to make love to him?

"You won't be I will be on the next deck."

"I hate you being so far away."

"Me too, but it is only for a few days."

"You're right, I can make this work." They had shared hotel rooms but had yet to sleep together and her feelings had skyrocketed in that time.

"Okay, now that that has been established, I don't want you to come out of this room unless I come to get you. This ship is full of men and I hope we don't have to have that discussion again."

"I can take care of myself, but I will obey. Can you come often; I am going to get so bored."

"Sure, but don't open up to anyone except me, okay?"

"Okay, Captain," she giggled.

. . ⚘ . .

TRUE TO HIS WORD SETH had taken Airy on walks, sat on the deck, and they shared their meals in private. They were able to experience each other with no interference. They had shared many small kisses and a few passionate ones since leaving the hospital, but tonight on the deck in the moonlight, as he watched her, he couldn't hold back any longer. Seth caressed Airy's face, and she tilted her head loving the feel of his hand on her. His thumb rubbed her ruby lips and quickly his mouth descended on hers. Their kiss instantly became feverish as his hands roamed her body. He felt their heat combining and wanted nothing more than to make love to her. But hearing men approach he realized that this wasn't the place for a romantic interlude.

"Airy, let's get out of here," he breathed in her ear after ending their kiss. Taking her hand, he led her back to her tiny little room. The two narrowly made it inside before they began undressing the other. Intense kisses took them to the bed and before Seth lay down beside Airy, he said, "I want you with all of me but this isn't something that needs to be rushed."

"Seth, I've desired you for a long time but I didn't want to push."

He smiled, "If I'd known that you wouldn't have been in this twin bed the past two nights without me."

Settling himself beside Airy, he began his assault of passionate kisses again trailing them from her lips down her neck and back up again before he slowly began to take her entire body to the pinnacle point where passion and love collide.

· · ❦ · ·

TWO MONTHS OF HIDING from authorities, family, and the scientific community only strengthened the bond between Seth and Airy but did not give them peace to live a life that wasn't on the run, though the conflict continued to stand between them. As long as they talked and interacted on other subjects, they were very much harmonious. She still believed she possessed a moral responsibility; however, she also saw what havoc telling her truth would unleash.

Seth sipped his coffee deep in thought, they were in Australia at a small house on the beach. He'd experienced something incredible but wasn't certain he could believe what that meant and if he should tell Airy about the past few weeks.

"Seth, I am feeling cooped up may we go to town? Don't you think by now things will be back to normal after all the news hasn't reported anything about Africa or the object after they finally removed it?"

"True, I have kept in touch with Stephen through my parents and nothing has been reported since his exorcism from the project after extracting the globe. I believe we should remain under the radar."

"Do you think anyone else experienced the same thing as I did? No reports have come out or any rumors as far as we know."

"I don't think we are in a position to hear any news of that sort. The fact that the public doesn't know anything other than a sphere was found on the side of Mt. Nimba may mean you are safe; however, for now, I believe we shouldn't take precautions with your safety."

"I hate that you tanked your reputation because of me."

He put his coffee cup down on the counter and walked over to her, lovingly placing his first two fingers under her chin so that she would look up at him and spoke, "I told you the day we left the hospital that you mean the world to me and I would do whatever was needed to make sure you were safe and I don't regret any of it."

"Including the time in solitude?"

"Especially not the time in solitude." He smiled a devilishly charming smile at her and she knew he was thinking about the nights and days of passion that they shared the past months.

"Stop that right now, we just got out of bed and it is nearly noon sometimes I think you have a one-track mind."

"Only when my eyes look upon you, Darling." He licked his upper lip as if anticipating their next kiss and when Airy watched him do so she couldn't help the grin that formed on her as well. However, neither needed to wait because they were in each other's arms as soon as the spark ignited.

Seth's lips took full possession of Airy's. His hands roamed her back before going to the nape of her neck and lovingly caressing the area. He began to remove her lightweight green sweater on her right shoulder, applying the spot with warm kisses.

Airy felt a tingling sensation build within her loins, her legs weakened. She clung to Seth's body with arms fastened around his neck, while her fingers played with the long deep brown hair at his nape. The aroma of zest body wash and coffee clung to him. His head was now below her lips and she placed kisses along his temple tasting the saltiness of his skin.

He lowered his body more placed his arm beneath her knees and picked her up carrying her away to the room they shared. Depositing her lightly on the bed he climbs in on top kissing her fervently, driving them both to their passion edge. Suddenly the phone rang startling them both. Seth jumps up to answer it as if it were a fire needing extinguished.

He glanced at it, 'unknown caller,' he tensely said, "Hello."

"Hello, Mate, this is Zack I know we haven't talked in a while and I was hoping you could meet me. Yea, Mate, I know it has been some time but since I'm back in my home town I was hoping we could get together at the usual place. Maybe even have those pancakes and omelets again, see you there, same time as usual."

Seth looked at the phone for a second and then put it down.

"Was it your dad? You didn't say anything."

"No, it wasn't Dad or Uncle Stephen it was Zack."

"Zack as in the geologist?"

"Yeah."

"How did he get the burner phone number?"

"I don't know only my father has it. Even Uncle Stephen doesn't. And your parents have to call mine for information. It's strange. I can't understand why my father would give it out. It must have been important."

"What did he say?"

"That also was strange and I believe he meant for it to be coded, something that he and I are familiar with."

"Don't leave me hanging what did he say?"

"To meet him, at a restaurant that we both previously went to."

"That's all?"

"Yeap."

"We have to return to Africa?"

"Well, no, he wants to meet me in Sydney."

"In Sydney are you certain?"

"I think. He said he was back in his home town and he grew up in Sydney and went to college there."

"Sydney's is a few hours away, right?"

"Yes, and he wants me to meet him at six tonight."

"Tonight?"

"Yes, I believe so, he mentioned us eating at a restaurant and said he'd like the same thing pancakes and omelets. There were only two places we ate the hotel and a pancake house, and we dined there at six in the evening and that is what we consumed."

"Ok, so Sydney must have a diner named that." Airy grabbed the burner phone and started typing, "So what's the name?"

"Joe's Crispy Flapjacks, I think."

"It's going to be hard to figure out which one there are three in Sydney."

"What street are they on?"

"One is on Nelly, then Smate, and the last one is on Fellowship Lane."

"That didn't work. What is nearby each?"

"Wait I need to pull up the map for that. Okay, the one on Nelly has two convenient stores nearby," Airy looked up and Seth who shook his head no. "The one on Fellowship has a taco place, an Island drinks and liquor store," She raised her head to meet Seth's smiling face. "So, Fellowship Lane it is."

. . ⚘ . .

"I'M NOT HAPPY THAT you didn't stay at the house, Airy. This could be dangerous. Zack could be forced or just setting us up. I only knew him a few days."

"You said he seemed like a good guy, not one that would steer you into a setup."

"Yes, but sometimes things aren't as they seem. For money people will turn on their family."

"So how about a code word or I could stay in the car and be your get-away driver? I just couldn't be over two hours away from you not knowing what was going on. If you never returned, I wouldn't know what happened and have no car to come look for you. After all, we were a bit isolated down by that wonderful secluded beach. Only you me and the sharks," she laughed to lighten the mood.

Seth loved her tiny laugh and she was right if anything went wrong, she wouldn't know who or how or even if he was dead. "Ok, you stay in the car if the situation seems good, I will text your phone. Will that work for you?"

"Yes, and a kiss will do," she purred.

"Okay, remember to stay here no matter what. If something transpires call my dad and only say red flag and you're safe. He will know you are going to a backup destination; he doesn't know it but knows who to contact for that information. I will come as soon as I can, okay?"

"Yes, and be careful. I love you," she smiled.

"What did you say?"

"I love you."

His face flashed a broad grin before he leaned back in the car and kissed her. The union was brief, however in those few moments he showed her such warmth and passion taking the time to caress her face as he deepened their kiss. He longed to hear her say she loved him. He wanted to tell her so many times, but he was going through something that he couldn't tell her or anyone about just yet. It was confusing and frightening and a few times he wanted to take her away from their little bungalow, although he felt a need to see what he was experiencing through to the end. "You are my life now and I am completely yours so I'll fight Satan himself to make sure we have a life together."

Her eyes were liquid with desire, "I will hold you to that Mr. Lock."

Seth placed a baseball hat on his head, making sure his now long hair lay outside the cap. Placing a pair of sunglasses on to hide his appearance further hoping that if this was a setup he wouldn't be recognized. He sat down at the counter and the waitress handed him a menu poured a glass of water then walked off. Seth pretended to look at the menu as he used the over-the-counter mirror to view the room behind him. Zack was at a corner table looking around nervously. He would expect this reaction so it didn't disturb him, however, he wanted to be certain there was no other reason for his behavior. He waited at the counter after ordering coffee and pie, watching Zack and the room. Ten minutes later he waved the waitress over, "Bring my food over to the corner table I just noticed the man there is a friend."

"Sure, and I'll bring you a fresh cup of coffee too," she said as she picked up his empty one.

"Thanks," he threw a twenty-dollar bill on the counter and walked toward Zack.

Zack noticed a man walking toward him who was sitting at the counter and began to panic. He wondered if he'd been followed.

Seth slid into the booth seat across from his friend and it wasn't until that moment that recognition spread across his colleague's face. "Are you sure this is safe?"

"I can't be one hundred percent with so many places having access to scans, cameras, and such but I made sure I wasn't followed and this place doesn't have any cameras inside or out, however, that being said we should make this quick because you have been here a while. I didn't notice it was you at the counter or when you came over until you sat down."

"I thought as much. That means my disguise is working."

"Yeah, Mate. That long hair and shabby beard had me at a disadvantage."

"So, let's start with how did you get my number and knew we were nearby?"

"I called your Uncle Stephen, then met up with him, he is in the loop, but felt like he was being watched so he gave me your dad's burner phone number and the professor told him by the time I called that it was important. I know why all the cloak and dagger. You were right to hide her, but that day I couldn't understand, now I know more. At first, there were rumors that she experienced something harmful. Then she knew more than she should, circulated, and after we extricated the object, we handed it over to the military. I am sure your uncle told you as much. We were all let go and instructed not to divulge any information. A few weeks ago, they came at me asking questions, like what did I know, did I touch it without gloves, what did you say or what did I know of Miss Sheppard's interaction with it? I didn't know what to make of it, however, I have friends who work in a lot of different areas, government as well as scientific, once they started probing me, I became more inquisitive and what I found out is, that they needed Airy. She is the only one who has gotten anything from the artifact and they believe she did. They think it is a communication device and they want to know everything she does and they need her to make it work again."

"So, from what you've said she is in danger."

"You can look at it that way or that she is needed. Your uncle didn't tell me much about what she knew or experienced. However, what I have heard is it spoke to her and she knows things about our past. Things the government, military, and scientific community want to know although, I have also heard that this information is dangerous and they don't want knowledge of anything concerning it getting out. Mate, the main reason I needed to contact you was that they know you are somewhere in Australia. I am here to warn you and help get you out before they find you both."

"Zack, I have to ask is there something in this for you? Did they send you, are you helping them?"

"Mate, I can understand your thinking so I won't take offense, but I am here as a friend. Right now, I think you could use that. We need to go get Airy; I know a place deep in the outback they will never find you. You can stay there until I come for you."

Seth was considering everything Zack told him and it all seemed plausible but something in the back of his mind whispered that this man was taking a hell of a chance for virtual strangers. He'd feel better taking matters into his own hands than involving someone in what could be risky circumstances. Though did he have a choice? He questioned himself before his phone buzzed. He looked down and it was Airy.

"2 black SUVs just pulled up. Get out now, back entrance."

"You set me up!" Seth jumped up looked around and started running toward the kitchen where he knew the back door would be.

Zack also jumped up, "What? I didn't," he tried to grab Seth's arm but missed. He began to follow behind him.

Seth rushed through the kitchen door and people within started screaming at him, "You can't be back here!" He didn't slow down as he made his way pushing people aside and rushing for the door.

Just outside he saw the car and Airy then Zack grabbed him from behind. With quick reflexes, he turned and slammed his fist into Zack's midsection. Breathless Zack tried to tell him it wasn't him. Seth was almost to the car by the time Zack yelled, "Go I will distract them. Go now!"

Seth opened the car door and stepped in though before he made it inside one of the black SUV's pulled up in front of them. Airy put the car in reverse as he climbed in and pushed hard on the gas pedal and just as she turned the car around the other SUV was in front of her new position blocking them. Seth cursed and said, "Don't say anything Airy, act like you no longer remember anything. Understand?"

Airy nodded as the man in the passenger seat in front of them got out of the car and began his aggressive walk toward them.

Seth looked toward Zack for a brief second and saw two men standing behind him with their hands on his upper arms holding him in place.

"Seth Lock, Airy Sheppard you are wanted by the African military we are here to take you to the Embassy."

Seth felt a little confused. The men before him were Americans and they said they were taking them to the Embassy in Africa, the American Embassy.

Chapter Nine

"Why won't they talk to us?" Airy questioned Seth with distress.

"I think these men are just doing their job of recovering us and escorting us to Africa. Right, Zack?" He said looking at the only other passenger in the back area of the plane. The officers were five seats away toward the front of the jet.

"What can I say that I haven't already? This wasn't my doing."

Seth made a grunting noise before he looked at Airy. "We should try and get a little rest while we wait."

. . ~ . .

"I TOLD YOU I DON'T remember anything. The doctors said I was dreaming," Airy answered their question for the ninth time.

"Stop stalling and tell us what you know."

"I can't tell you anything more. I simply don't have any knowledge of anything from that hospital stay, or before. You have been asking me for hours and I already told you I want a lawyer."

"You don't need one you are not under arrest."

"Then release me now!"

A large man with a balding crown stepped into the room and motioned with his head for the younger man dressed in a black suit to leave along with his companion, who was also attired in all black. He turned the chair in front of Airy backward and sat his heavy frame down. "Miss Sheppard, my name is General David Turner and I work for the government of the United States. I want to be open and upfront with you. The African military believes you have knowledge of something that they are not willing to share with us, though they expect us to just hand you over to them. That will not be happening without more information and we were hoping you could provide us with that. I have investigated what they told us about you and Mr. Lock working on a project for their government and they said you were rushed to the hospital and you both left their employment abruptly and they feel you have taken knowledge that somehow is significant to their scientist. I am just asking for your full cooperation to make certain they do not mean you any harm."

"I thank you for at least explaining that much since none of the others did more than ask me what I know."

"I am sorry for my co-worker's lack of conduct and patience. So do you think you can help?"

"Mr. Lock should be privy to our conversation."

"That can be arranged. I will have them take you back to the waiting room we've supplied for you, and some food was brought in for fortification, we can talk afterward." He stood and walked to the door, "Oh, by the way, I will arrange for Mr. Lock and Mr. Patton to join you for dinner."

Turner sent in an array of food items and Seth arrived soon after. Airy jumped up and ran into his arms when he walked through the door. Kissing her feverishly he asked breathlessly, "Are you okay? They didn't harm you?"

"No, they have been basic gentlemen other than all the questions."

Seth hugged her tightly again needing to feel her safe in his arms and whispered in her ear, "Did you tell them?"

She kissed his mouth and murmured, "No. But they say I need to tell them so they can help. That the African military wouldn't disclose why they wanted us."

"Us?"

"Yes. A mister Turner said we would all talk later."

He whispered again, "Let me do the talking."

Airy shook her head glad to hand him the pressure, "I was worried about you."

"You were worried about me? Darling, I went out of my mind and have been hatching a plan to jump the men guarding my room. I was moments away from coming to find you."

They walked toward the table when the door opened and Zack was pushed inside. "Man, what the hell happened to you?" Seth asked gaping at him.

"They didn't like the way I answered their questions after I tried to escape."

"You tried to get away?" Airy questioned.

"Yeah, when we first got here, one of the men guarding me turned his back, I kicked him to the ground and I jumped the other man. I was winning for a while."

"So, that's when they beat you up?" Seth wanted to know.

"That and when they asked what I was doing at the diner I kinda told him to go screw his mother. I think he protested a little too much," Zack snickered in pain.

"Come sit down and let me put some ice on that eye," Airy insisted.

"Thanks, but I think I'd rather gnaw on a piece of that fried chicken. I am starved."

· · ✿ · ·

"I HOPE THE FOOD WAS satisfactory," Turner questioned when he came to the room after they finished eating and the food was cleared away. "Now if we can get down to what you know that makes the military in Africa so nervous."

Zack, Airy, and Seth sat down at the long table. Seth spoke first and asked, "Suppose you tell us everything they told you why they demanded our presence back here, then we can fill in the rest." Seth had no intention of telling them everything, however, they needed to start somewhere.

"Okay, I assume that is fair." He relayed what they knew of the situation and it wasn't much more than he'd told Airy.

"So, what are you wanting from us and why?" Seth questioned.

"We need to know why they want you so badly. What was entailed on the project?"

Seth saw no destruction in telling him what they knew of the venture. "We were told an earthquake occurred and that something was down inside the mountain cavity which they wanted us to find and extract."

"Yes, that's the same information we were given."

"But there is more to it. You see once the seismologists arrived, they realized it wasn't an earthquake that created the hole and the geologist suspected it was a little like an explosion but not quite. Deep down the moderately stable hole, we saw a kaleidoscope of lights coming from the impression of the mountain. When at last we found the area there was a rock-type object inside and when Airy touched it she was shocked, for lack of a better word, and hurt so bad she ended up in a coma."

"So, are you saying this is something alien?"

"No, we don't know what it is," Zach chimed in.

"So, why do they want you and Miss Sheppard so much? What happened to her has something to do with it?"

"I guess," Seth answered.

"Miss Sheppard, what exactly did you experience?"

"I don't remember anything."

"Yes, that is what you said earlier however, I find it hard to believe that they would request so adamantly your return if there were not something else going on. And why would you have been on the run?"

"Look, Man, we have told you everything. Can we go now?" Zack stated angrily.

"No, I need to talk to the African government officials and their military first and let them know we are not going to hand you over unless you have committed some sort of crime. It is not our government's way," he stood and left the room.

After several minutes a man came in and said, "I will escort you to your rooms for tonight please follow me."

The three reluctantly followed the man out and to a jeep outside and from there they were taken to a separate building in the back which looked a lot like a hotel. The man opened the door escorted them inside and said we only have two rooms available so Miss Sheppard this is yours and the room next door the men can share. If you need anything there is an in-house phone that goes directly to the front desk, gentlemen this way please."

Once inside the room, Seth opened the adjoining door to Airy's room. He whispered to Zack to look for listening devices everywhere and he did the same in Airy's room. After they found none Seth turned on the TV loudly and motioned for the others to join him at the table. "I think it is safe to talk."

"So how do we proceed?" Zack wanted to know.

"First, we should talk this through and sort out anything we can that might aid in our release," Seth answered.

"I thought that's what we just did," Airy voiced.

"We'll it didn't exactly aid in our release and if I read Turner right, I don't believe he has any intentions on letting us go just yet."

"Since most of the stuff he wanted to know has nothing to do with me I can't see why he hasn't freed me," Zack voiced.

"Because you were at the dig site also, I think he feels you're privy to everything that went on and hoping you can give information we haven't."

"Is there more information to give? Are you telling me and him everything?" Reading the looks on Seth's and Airy's faces he asked, "What don't I know guys, I think after what I've been through you could help a mate out and at least tell me what's going on?"

The two lovers looked at one another, still unsure telling what they knew was a good idea and whether they could trust Zack. "Seth, I think it would be wise to fill him in on what happened and let him make up his own mind."

"If I let Airy explain you must promise not to say anything because we don't know for certain this is fact and it could possibly get us killed. I am putting my trust in you. Don't let me down Zack, this could mean ours, and I include you once we tell you, our deaths." Seth hoped he was reading Zack right and he wasn't working with these men, after all, they did beat him up.

"I know it may not be true," Airy said still feeling assaulted and finding it hard to understand why after all their talks Seth couldn't believe her.

Zack agreed and Airy told him everything she experienced in the coma and when she was done Zack just looked at her in wonder for a few minutes before he spoke. "You are saying that everything, everything, we know of as our past is wrong that some other beings were here on earth long ago and we have their genetic makeup, however, they are so advanced they left earth and still come back like the ancient alien theories. That humanity is genetically their link. God never existed and therefore religious practices are to no God. We advanced too slowly so they abandoned us, and they have come back to help us now. What do they want from us?"

"I don't know all the ins and outs just yet, but they seemed like they want us to know now since, they feel we can handle the information about our past and help us with something they said was destructive to our world."

"Seth, you believe this is bull shit?"

"I.... Everything we as people have proven of how the earth developed, and of how man came to be, or what we take as proof says the possibility is there. Add all the artifacts lately that have been found that are out of place for primitive man; as well as the skeletal evidence that has been produced lately that dates further and further back in time, the building of the pyramids. I can't rule this out just yet. This needs lots of investigation and we may never have the answers."

"Look this is beyond us. I mean we have to... I mean shouldn't we tell them? It's not up to us to make this huge decision."

"That may be true, however, if we tell the world what happens then? Chaos. I don't know the right thing that is why I took Airy and hid from the world hoping the African government would be able to sort this out. Airy was in danger because she told the doctors, priest, and a few nurses and such heard her speak of this. I was convinced by the way the priest and bishop at that hospital looked at her they feared what she said. This could lead to a religious shutdown and they weren't going to allow that."

"I get that and all but the flip side is if all this is true how can we turn a blind eye to the most significant discovery in the human race? From what you said there is more discovery to come. Besides all that, this is a career maker for you two and maybe myself."

"Zack, you said you would keep our confidence," Airy said as Seth stood with his fist knotted ready to pound some sense into his former partner.

Putting up his hands as he stood backing away, he said, "I did and I want to but I also have a strong feeling we should allow the world the opportunity to come to their own conclusions. Who are we to play, for lack of a better word, God?"

"That's not what's going on here. We don't know if this is true. This is something that could change our whole existence. What if this thing was planted and it has been rigged to give this false information, it could all be a hoax or Airy may have just dreamt while in a coma."

The door soared open and with it, two men wearing black suits rushed in, one grabbed Seth and handcuffed him while the other seized Airy forcefully, she pushed and screamed trying to free herself.

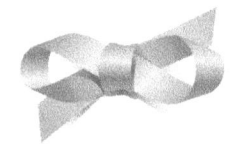

Chapter Ten

For the past week, Airy was questioned daily by African officials. For the most part, she didn't vary from her original story until they brought in the recording of her and Seth's talk with Zack. It was a little hard to hear at times but it laid out what was said enough that she could no longer dispute what she told him. Why had they trusted Zack? He must have been wearing a recording device, just as Seth thought he was deceiving them. With no choice, she explained everything she knew and finished again with it may not be anything more than a dream state while she was comatose. But she knew they didn't believe her. Her instincts said they knew something more they weren't saying.

A knock at the door brought about trepidation as she lifted herself from the black reclining chair, by the solitary table and bed in the tiny room where they held her prisoner. She didn't ask who was there because it didn't matter, it was assuredly the same people it had been every day for the past week.

The door opened to the dimly lit hall and a woman came in. "Here is your breakfast miss and I have been given this change of clothing for you. In thirty minutes, I will return to take you to the showers so you can freshen up. You are to see the man in charge today."

"Why?"

"He hopes you can help with a problem. He is very thrilled to have you aid him. Well, that is the talk I have heard anyhow."

The girl was increasingly friendly as the week wore on, though Airy missed Seth and her family too much to allow anything to add pleasure to her mood.

After a needed shower she felt at last ready to see how she could possibly help. More questions she mused as she placed the clothing that they gave her earlier on.

When she first arrived, she found a pack of cards and a 5000-piece puzzle on the small table to keep her busy. Being a prisoner seemed more like being at camp on a rainy day except with no friends, and communication only with her captures and their many questions.

After another thirty minutes, a knock at the door again made her rise from the reclining chair. The door opened the same young woman directed her outside to the hall where two armed guards escorted them the same way, as usual, she thought to herself. To her surprise they didn't stop at the interrogation room, at least that's how she considered it. They passed through several doors and then exited the building.

Light from the sun shined on her face for the first time in a week and she couldn't help but pause for a moment to soak it in. She didn't realize how much she'd missed the heat penetrating her skin. Though with that warmth came the memory of Seth, his warm brown eyes that always looked at her with such tenderness. His soft heated kisses that caressed her body, and his deep baritone voice that she couldn't get enough of. She missed his affection, his smile, his scent, the touch of his hand, and his very presence in her life. She dreamt every night about making love to him, about their talks of life, and even about the object that created this mess in their lives. She wanted to scream, no more, let me go so I can be with the man I love. She prayed for his safety. She asked about him the first few days though her only answer was that he is doing what we ask and as long as he does, he will not be harmed. What that meant she had no idea; however, she knew they didn't want to harm them they were searching for information.

They went by three buildings and went inside the fourth and last one. It only contained two rooms and an elevator the guards stayed as she and the girl boarded the lift and the girl pressed the basement level on the wall pad, there were only two other levels. The elevator made a clucking noise and the doors opened. The bright light shined the artificial glow of fluorescence. The girl led her toward the back of the room. They passed several workstations where people were occupied but she couldn't see what they were doing. Nearing the last area she caught sight of the rock object within a glass-type box that filtered its light and knew it was the item that set this whole situation into motion.

Airy stared at the object, internally she felt the electricity shoot through her, not nearly as intense as it was that day but she could feel the electrical pulse feet away from the stone. Her spine shivered as her eyes fixed on the object, then a touch on her shoulder startled her and she spun around to the tall man behind her. "Zack!"

"Yeah, it's amazing ain't it."

"You lying son of a bit.."

"Wait now, I am going to say it again. This wasn't me. I am here against my will like I assume you and Seth are. However, I decided to help as Seth is and hope they will let us go eventually and I presume that is why you are here in this lab."

"No, I was told and made to come."

"Yes, that was my doing. Hello, I am Dr. Howard Chase," he extended his hand to shake hers.

Airy didn't bother to respond, her glaring liquid green eyes speaking volumes.

He brushed past her, none reaction. "Miss Sheppard, it seems that you have something in common with a few people and that would be the occurrence of a set of numbers that have been making themselves known for some time to the world. With that realization, we have conducted some tests to gain more information than what you supplied."

"Have you been subjecting people to that thing?" she wanted to know.

"Well, yes, but not in the way you think. We have not made anyone touch the object, that didn't want to do so of their own volition."

Airy didn't realize she'd been holding her breath until that moment when she released it, now feeling relieved that no one was harmed. "Well, at least no one went through what I did, right?"

"Well, I would like to tell you that but at this point, I cannot. You must understand the people who stepped forward knew what was possible, we gave them the option and they chose for themselves and the stone did the same thing to them as it did to you."

"How many? How many people did you expose to it?"

"As of yesterday, four, and of the four one person died."

"Died!"

"Yes, I am sorry to say but this person did have underlying health issues that we believe contributed to his death."

"So just why am I here? What do you want from me that the others couldn't give you?"

"Ah, Mr. Lock you have come at the perfect time I was about to explain to Miss Sheppard why I need her assistance. You see Miss Sheppard the others who participated have since regained consciousness and it seems they also had what you called dreams of people that said they were of this earth. However, you are the only one so far that has a name for these people. So, we are inclined to believe you gained more communication with people from our past or more accurately our present."

"Okay, you believe me, now what?"

"Well, can you tell me how we are to gather more information?"

"No."

"We have tried many things to gain access from radio frequencies, vibration, temperature variations, water, radiation, hitting it with hammers even, and more. So, if you think about it, I believe there is only one way."

"No! You aren't suggesting that I touch it again? It's liable to kill me this time."

"Miss Sheppard, you know as well as I there are always risks in life and some are more important than others. I feel like this is worth taking that chance."

"No, I won't. You can't make m..." Airy stopped suddenly when Seth was pushed forward by gunpoint. Where had the guards come from? Were they there all along? She suddenly felt light-headed, and sick to her stomach.

"This information could change the world as we know it, not just what we believe as our past. We need to know these answers. What you do will go down in history."

"May I have a few minutes alone with Miss Sheppard to get her to see why doing this will be the best for all involved?" Seth questioned.

"I suppose cooperation is worth a little time." Dr. Chase directed everyone around to step away with him, after all, he wasn't worried, they would try and leave with the armed guards in the room.

Seth stepped closer to Airy and with a low voice he said, "Are you okay they haven't hurt you or anything?"

"No, it has just been torture being away from you, not knowing how you were if they..."

"Yeah, same here," he said cutting her off and glancing behind himself. "Airy I have been doing my best to help them to gain our release, but nothing we did accomplish any results."

"Why would you help...?"

"Just listen, they began right away fixed on the numbers, the people who experienced them. Then those people apparently reacted as you did. Zack and others touched it and nothing, but when the people like you who knew the coordinates lay their hands on the orb the lights beamed such brightness outward that all in the room had to turn away. The electrical charge that occurred threw each person across the room. I was shown a film and it was unreal. I could imagine how it had hurt you."

"If I do it again, Seth," Airy stated panicked.

"I know, but I need you to stall them so I can get us outa here."

"How?"

"Well, I have been considering that and we haven't been in touch with family so I think if you asked to see your parents first, you know in case this kills you, they may allow it."

"Bring my parents here and expose them to this danger."

"I don't think they will come if you aren't the one reaching out, but if they do it will take a few days."

"No, I can't."

"Airy, you don't have a choice. They mean to have answers and they don't care if you are killed, they will just find someone else, they are now desperate. They are hoping that you somehow have a better chance than the others of making this thing work, after all, you gained more knowledge though you were also in a comatose state longer."

"So, what do you think is the likelihood of this thing not killing me?"

"I'd say good, but it's an estimate. I don't want you to take the chance though. It communicated with you, so believe it wasn't made to be harmful, bu..."

"Okay, I hope you are ready," Dr. Chase stated walking up beside Seth.

"Before I agree may I ask to talk to my parents on the phone first?"

"For what reason?"

"Well, I think if I die doing this then it was the very least you the government and military here could have done is allow me one last time to tell my parents that I love them."

"I will see, I will have the guards return you to your room while I wait for word."

"I'd like to stay here and read your notes on everything you have tried if that is okay."

"Well, I suppose that would be fine, but the guards stay."

"Can Mr. Lock and anyone else who has worked on the project stay in case I have questions?"

"I suppose," he said before waving over the military men and advising them to keep everyone in this room till he returned.

"Okay, Seth, I bought us at least a few minutes what do we do now?"

Looking around the room, Seth felt deflated he could think of nothing to get them out of this jam. The doctor's assistant walked toward them carrying an armload of files. Zack was talking to another scientist across the room and the guards were about five feet away from them looking in their direction off and on. Another three men and a woman were working at stations so they were not paying them any attention. If they made a run for it precisely how far would they get? There were buildings and people all around outside this room, and they would have to take the elevator up then more guards. No, there was no way an escape would work from here, but he noticed the bottle of acid on the table beside him and it gave him an idea.

"Here is all the research Miss Sheppard if I can explain anything further, please let me know." Sitting the folders on the table by Airy the assistant turned and walked away.

"I have a plan; I just need you to stall them till morning and be ready tonight." He glanced again at the bottle beside him hoping Airy would follow his motion and understand what he would do.

Airy shook her head acknowledging she understood and then sat down to start reading one file after the next and prayed Seth and she would be free tonight. Luckily, they were told that Airy could call home that evening and they could pick up the following morning with the sphere.

· · ⚓ · ·

MIDNIGHT AND STILL no sign of Seth. She worried all evening if this plan was a good idea, after all, there were armed guards stationed around and locked doors everywhere. The vial of acid was small it couldn't possibly undo every lock they needed to escape, but she trusted Seth with everything in her.

She heard a soft tap at the door and anticipation with a hint of dread leaped in her chest. Within seconds Airy began to cough and she realized she was standing too close to the door, and though this acid didn't smell like Hydrogen sulfide acid it did release a potent gas, making her cover her mouth and nose with the sleeve of her sweater and step back toward the small bed. Several long minutes later the locked door clicked and Seth walked in. Airy abandoned her position at the side of the bed and ran to him springing into his arms. She kissed him with so much passion that it fogged his brain making him forget for numerous minutes his mission to get them out.

Stepping back from Airy finally he asked, "You ready?"

She nodded, and stated, "Is this plan going to work?"

"I sure hope so." He would like to have told her yes with certainty but he knew that the changes were less than fifty percent, but he couldn't sit back and let them force her to touch that globe again. He couldn't stomach losing her not after he found the other half of his soul. He placed another shorter kiss on her red warm lips, the lips he loved to touch. He'd missed her so much it hurt in the past week that they were kept separate. Touching her cheek with his hand he whispered, "Ready, and be very quiet."

Chapter Eleven

They slid out of her room and down the hall to the doorway at the end. Seth worked quickly on the lock and the one in the next corridor. By that time there was scarcely enough left in the vial to continue and he knew there were two more locked areas before they would merge outside of the building. Apprehension plagued Seth as he motioned for Airy to walk silently behind him. He went to work on the lock with the little acid left in the vial. Trying to get the fluid in the dropper, he'd also taken, proved to be difficult. With what minuscule he recovered Seth placed it on the locking mechanism praying it worked. The acid took longer than he anticipated but at last, the latch clicked, but to his surprise, it wasn't from the acid.

The door swung open and on the opposite side, there stood two guards and Zack. "So, you never planned to help? Well, I guess that's why we devised so many precautions to make sure this wouldn't transpire, however, we never assumed you would get this far."

"Zack," Airy gasped in surprise.

"Yeah, the pretense is over. I have been working for the African military all along. I tried playing your friend but now I will have to play rough."

"You son of a bitch!" Seth balled up his fist to punch Zach but one of the guards slammed the butt of his rifle into Seth's stomach making him bend over in pain.

"Like I said now I have to be harsh. Airy, if you will come with me, we can finally get the answers?" He motioned for her to go before him and told the other guard to go wake Dr. Chase. He then gestured for the guard that hit Seth, who was still holding his gut, to bring him along.

Airy took a few paces then stopped and turned back to Zack, "Why? You know that thing is likely to kill me at the very least I'll be in a coma again."

"If you can give them answers it doesn't matter to me. I just want the money they promised."

"Money! Life doesn't matter, the world doesn't matter, just you."

"Yep, Honey. When it comes to half a million nothing else matters. Get moving," he pushed her forward.

Seth reacted, gun or not he wasn't going to let them hurt the woman he loved. He seized Zack from behind and launched him toward the guard. He grabbed Airy's arm and began to run not knowing if they would shoot but betting, they weren't going to harm the only one they thought could get them answers.

The two men gained control of their bodies after falling to the floor and took off after their prisoners. They saw them make a right turn down another hall and then a left which led to a row of rooms, most were office spaces, and when they rounded the corner Airy and Seth were nowhere. They began looking into each room one at a time.

Seth pushed Airy into a room and he quickly looked for a hiding place. There was a partition he motioned toward it as he locked the knob on the door softly. Airy ran behind it and then Seth. "What are we going to do, they will find us here?"

Seth looked around and noticed a panel at the base of the wall behind them. It was small and looked like a duct space, he hoped it would lead somewhere, but taking it was their only chance. He knelt, unlatched the hinge, and motioned for Airy to go inside. He followed her, though first, he hauled a large box, heavier than he would have liked, over toward the door and pulled it to the hole right after he got inside. Which made him have to back his way into the tunnel-like opening as he struggled to shut the panel from within.

Inside Airy slid on her stomach in the dark pushing away spider webs as she went. Soon the cramped space came to a junction, she couldn't see but felt Seth behind her. "Which way?" she whispered.

"Go left maybe that will lead us to the outside wall." At the intersection, Seth contorted his body banging his head, legs, and arms on the walls to follow Airy, head forward.

They were in the tunnel-like space for nearly twenty minutes and Airy was afraid they'd never find a way out. Her palms were sweaty, the air stale, and she felt nausea begin to overtake her. Stopping, she breathed in and out through her nose a few times to settle herself.

Airy was stationary, Seth could hear her take deep breaths. Placing a hand on her foot he said, "You're okay. Airy, you are strong you can do this. We can get out just continue, and think of being free," he encouraged.

She took another breath and moved forward and soon she noticed a brightness in the distance. There was a grate on the wall and light spilled into their small space. Maneuvering herself she looked out of the opening. Relief washed through her; they were liberated at last. Seeing no one she pushed the metal screen and spilled out onto the earth.

Seth followed doing the same and quickly standing he looked around them. They were in a parking area. Military jeeps and large trucks, along with civilian cars lay before them. Although none of them would aid their escape without keys. Before he could think more, he heard voices nearby, "Airy run." He pulled on her as he ran for a large army truck with a tarp covering the back. They ducked down by the big wheels in the front while two men dressed in fatigues walked toward a group of jeeps. They climbed in one started it and took off. Seth felt his heart ease as they raced away. "Airy we must find a vehicle with keys if we want to get away. Stay low and go toward the personal cars. I'll look through the military ones, be quiet and careful in the dark."

Airy's head bobbed in acknowledgment. For the next ten minutes, they pulled on doors and looked through the windows of vehicles as best as they could praying just one would help them escape. Airy came up empty and was making her way back to Seth when from behind a man pulled on her arm forcing her out of her crouched position. Just then she heard the roar of an engine. She turned toward the noise and saw a Utility truck coming toward her with bright lights beaming. Turning back in the direction of the man that held her arm she kneed him hard in the privates and pulled with all her might to get free. She ran for the truck. A shot rang out, panic racing through her chest Airy stopped suddenly.

Seth heard the shot and caught sight of Airy as she stood still in the parking lot. The truck swerved and Seth tried to gain control. The front tire was shot and quickly deflated. It took a lot of effort before Seth could bring the massive vehicle to a complete stop without crashing into anything.

The man stood behind Airy with his gun pointed at her, "You in the truck get out now," he yelled.

Seth complied walking toward him with his hands in the air. "If you knew what this was all about, I know you would let us both go. I am only trying to keep them from killing her."

"My job is not to question," he responded his thick English accent coming to the surface.

"Maybe not," Airy turned toward him, "but is it to kill, because that is what is going to happen to me and they don't even know if my death is going to give them answers. Do you want to be a part of outright murder? Do you want my death on your conscious?"

"Look lady, I don't know what you are talking about. For all I know you are lying to me."

Seth halted his movements just in front of Airy and said, "She is not lying they want her to touch that glowing object in the lab, that was dug out of Mt. Nimba a few months ago. The last time it put her in a coma for weeks and this time it will probably kill her."

"Shut up and walk now," he ordered. Pressing the button on the walkie-talkie that was holstered to the front of his shirt near his left shoulder, he said, "This is Ellhart, I have the suspects in the parking area."

"Bring them to building 4's office on the double," Zack stated over the walkie.

"You heard him now go," the officer pointed towards the building to the right. They all started walking with Ellhart behind them with his gun pointing at Airy.

They walked slowly and continued to talk to the officer hoping to convince him to let them go before it was too late. As they approached building four Zack came out with the two guards from before, who were holding handcuffs.

"Since I can't seem to trust you two to behave then restrains will be used," Zack said with scorn.

Again, they were led to the elevators that went down to the labs in the basement. Seth felt conquered, but there was a small inkling he could save Airy if they would accept it. The one thing he hadn't used because he knew it wasn't likely to work.

The elevator hummed as it carried them downward, Seth could see the terror on Airy's face. He smiled his warmest smile letting his brown eyes say how much he loved her before he spoke softly, "Trust me, Airy, everything is going to be all right."

Airy tried to smile back letting him know that she trusted him, but she knew he couldn't save her. What happened next was beyond their control and she wished he didn't have to be there to see it. She could feel his love and with everything in her, she didn't want him to suffer. To see her die if that was her fate. She tried to tell herself that the Kabyars wouldn't send something that would give them information and then turn around and kill her with the same technology. However, she also knew that if it did kill her, it would be because her human body was just too fragile and the Kabyars hadn't anticipated that factor.

The elevator stopped and they were pushed out into the hall of the lab that contained the sphere. Anxiety raced through both Seth and Airy as their captures herded them ever closer to their doom.

Dr. Chase spoke as he neared the object, "I will need you to embrace the sphere not just touch it."

"How do I do that?" Airy questioned.

"Well, you will need to grip it with both hands."

"Wait!" Seth interrupted, "I haven't told anybody this but I have also touched the object and it didn't put me into a coma." All eyes were on him when he finished speaking. Pausing for a few seconds while they digested that information, he then began his explanation. "After Airy suffered the coma, I went back to the site this is when I began working with Zack. We worked to pry the damn thing out for days and once when Zack took a break and went to relieve himself, I stayed. I was so angry that Airy had been hurt badly that I decided to touch it. I thought if it killed me it didn't matter, at least I wouldn't feel accountable anymore. Anyway, I touched the vile thing."

"You what? But you didn't believe me," Airy choked out with a flash of anger.

"Let me finish, Airy. I was shocked and thrown backward just as you had been, but I didn't end up in a coma like you."

"You know what she knows?" questioned Dr. Chase.

"Yes, but my experience was different. You see while Airy lay comatose, she dreamt of this civilization long ago. With me, nothing happened at first. Even when Airy told me what happened I had no experience. It was nearly a week before things would just pop into my head, things that were similar to what Airy told me. She saw things and I just knew things. I feel what they were like as a people and how intelligent they are and were before.

The Kabyars were millions of years ahead of where we are now. This was before they even went to space. I suppose you can say they are so advanced now it would be like us comparing ourselves to cavemen.

They didn't spend their time doing anything that didn't better their minds or that distracted them from knowledge. They worked together as a community to better themselves and shared everything including living quarters, and what they ate. They spent their lives thinking, mastering, and being philosophers, as well as gaining new technology. They were driven by knowledge to always strive for more. Continuously driven forward to be more, to be better always evolving. You have to understand when they lived here on Earth their bodies were not the same as ours. They lived longer lives and didn't multiply as quickly as we do. They didn't breathe the same air as we do today, the planet was vastly different. Their brain capacity is larger.

They knew long before the asteroid that killed the dinosaurs came, they may have to leave the Earth. Earth's atmosphere was changing, and their breathing could only be helped with the use of apparatuses. The earth was violent with volcanic activity and earthquakes, dust that was so thick it was hard to see. They built many, many large ships. They had traveled farther in space by that time than we have today. They saw no other way to continue here so they soared away from the planet before they all died."

"Wait, why are you just now saying this when you could have told us all about them before?"

"For the same reason, I wouldn't let Airy tell anyone. This is something so complex that the world has to be eased into it. If we tell everyone what we know to be true about their life, about our ancestors. That life started here so long ago and God never created life, chaos would ensue. The Kabyars know this, that is why we have been given bits and pieces but no leaps in technology. We are children and have to learn like a child with fragments."

"I'm not buying what you're selling, Mate," Zack spit. "You are giving us information Airy knows, just stop this isn't going to work."

"I am being truthful." He was telling the truth about the information, but not as to how he gained the knowledge, or where the information came from. That was something he told no one about.

"Again, I say why now and not before we threatened her," he pointed at Airy.

"Because as I said, this doesn't need to go public."

"I know you, Mate, you would have spoken up earlier if it meant keeping her safe. Dr. Chase let's get on with this."

Considering what he heard Dr. Chase didn't know whom to believe. Since he needed information, whether, or not Mr. Lock was telling the truth, he must get all the answers, so he must have Miss Sheppard do her part. "Miss, if you would come sit down here," he pointed to a chair that had arm restraints on it.

"Don't I'm telling the truth," Seth shouted. He experienced dreams at the beach house that confirmed what Airy said, and a few things more. He didn't know why and yet as Airy he was certain they were authentic communications with the alien ancestors, without the use of the sphere.

Airy looked at Seth, she couldn't believe he'd experienced what she had and didn't tell her. He was holding this back all this time, and in all the instances he seemed far away deep in thought she now understood why. The strange look on his face when she would mention something new, she hadn't remembered before as if he knew what she was about to say, or that he simply was aware. He made her feel foolish at times for believing, she felt disheartened, and a surge of resentment for his betrayal. Her rage for his lack of trust for not believing mingled with her emotions of love and made her realize he never told her he loved her. He wasn't and had never loved her. In some peculiar way, he used her. Anger flashed inside and all she wanted was to get away from him and she possessed the opportunity at her fingertips. She could be strong and rid herself of his betrayal and at the same time help mankind discover more of its past by merging with the sphere. Seth's confession brought to light how hurtful people can be and her heart felt broken because she couldn't trust him anymore, could never trust him. The pain of the sphere was nothing compared to the hurt he showed her.

Airy slowly walked to the cold-looking chair and sat down, a guard removed the cuffs on her wrist. She didn't care anymore if she lived. There was no life without trust, respect, and love.

An eternity of time seemed to pass as Seth pleaded for them to stop; while Airy showed no hint of emotion, her now darkened eyes stared out blankly before her. A tear fell on her cheek for all she lost, all she never really possessed, and she couldn't help but identify with the world and what approached once everything came to light.

"Immediately after I secure these electrodes we will begin. I will need you to hold onto the sphere so the computer can register the data," the doctor said.

It took Dr. Chase several minutes to connect everything and, in that time, Seth tried to get Airy's attention. He wasn't certain of her thoughts, but he knew she was upset with him because she chose not to look at him once she sat in that blasted chair. It was a certainty that she would be disappointed that he never told her about his experiences with the ancestors, though he never considered she would be angry with him to the point she didn't fight what they were doing to her.

Seth tried to make her listen to him, make them end this but no one paid any attention. He struggled to get free and encountered another gun to his gut. He felt the air go out of his lungs as they lowered the sphere down to Airy's hands which were fastened vertically to the arms of the chair with leather straps, so as to hold them in place to grip the global object. They wanted to be certain she would not release quickly whether she or the sphere wanted her to.

Seth could feel the electrical impulses coming from the globe even at his distance of five feet away. The lights, of so many different colors, showed brighter the closer it got to Airy. He cried out again before her hands touched it. Her body convulsed. "It's killing her!" He screamed and slammed his shoulder into the guard that held him. The man went down on the floor as Seth's body charged forward. He collapsed onto her as an overpowering voltage hit him causing him to convul

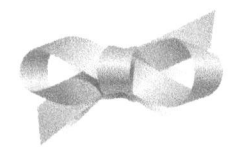

Chapter Twelve

Airy scanned the room around her. There were three other beds and she was in the fourth. She felt a searing pain in her hands and looked down at palms which were blistered and red. At least she thought to herself, they had the decency to place sab on the burns. Her wrists were in restraints that held her to the bed. Her head pounded like she had spent the night at a concert listening to music that blasted from large speakers.

Closing her eyes again she heard a moan coming from the bed beside her. She barely acknowledged the bump in it before closing her eyes. She knew that the man in the bed must be okay because she'd hardly been injured, besides that she didn't want anything to do with him. He betrayed her in horrendous ways: using her, lying, and denying her his love; a love she wanted but could never have. She felt the loss deeply and knew her heart would never heal, unlike her hands.

Gradually and with some effort Seth's eyes fluttered open. He surveyed the room before him noticing Airy's head turn away when he glanced in her direction. His heart was heavy knowing he'd hurt her at least that was what she felt. With a softness to his baritone voice, he asked "Airy, please look at me." With no response, he tried again, "You have every right to be upset with what I said earlier though once I explain I know you will forgive me. I didn't mean to anger you but I…"

Seth was cut off when Dr. Chase walked into the room demanding their attention. "You are both awake good, good. My nerves have been on edge waiting for you to awake. Please tell me what you saw, what you know."

Neither answered. Airy turned away from him and her green watery eyes met Seth's for a fraction of a second before she looked down at the sheets on the bed. The doctor looked at one then the other. Grabbing a chair and scrapping it across the floor he sat down and exhaled, "I don't have all day. I demand that you tell me what new things the object revealed."

Airy groaned and said, "I saw much as I did before but with more detail. Their physical appearance, they showed us the ships they made, told us of their lives here before they left."

"Such as?" Dr. Chase asked impatiently.

Seth chimed in, "We saw what the planet they came here from looks like, though since I do not know much about astronomy, I can't tell you anything significant in that area. They did say again that they lived here before going to the stars and by here, I mean Africa though it wasn't just Africa then because the continents had only started to break apart. That was what was causing the changes and why they abandoned the earth. All the atmospheric changes and volcanic eruptions, the plates shifting causing earthquakes were more than their bodies could handle. For hundreds of years, they had already explored outside of our planet's atmosphere. The changes Earth would continue to go through for millions of years meant they had to leave."

"Did they tell you how we are related to them?"

This time Airy turned to the doctor and said, "They have done DNA testing on us in the past and we have some of their DNA markers, however, our code is vastly different than theirs and they speculate that somehow their DNA that remained on the planet was used in our forming many hundreds of thousands of years ago."

They filled the doctor in on what they could and after he felt as though he'd gathered all the information, he said, "I thank you both, I wished it had not taken the turn it did to gather the information but as I have said all along, we did not wish you any harm and you will be allowed to leave. However, only after we get a written statement from you both agreeing not to say anything to anyone about what you have been told by the sphere and to act as though you never heard of its existence and its location. What has taken place since your arrival here in Africa, before you even landed on Mt. Nimba, is now classified as top secret. Please for your own sake abide by this. In the future, there may be a time when this is public knowledge, who knows but for now, you will be silent or you will be picked up by our military and I do believe that is not a good thing."

Once Dr. Chase was gone Seth tried again with Airy and she continued to shut him off to the point that she screamed at him to leave her alone. He did as she asked hoping with time, she would forgive him. He did what he did to save her, his only regret was it didn't work. Also, he hated that he caused her distress over the secret he kept while at the little beach house.

They spent two more days in Africa before they were released and given tickets on a commercial plane back to the United States and Austin's Airport where they originally started this project. Once at the airport, they were left alone to board the plane. Airy sat across from Seth as they awaited their flight. He tried several times to talk to her and after a while, she got up and took a seat a few rows from him. He wasn't going to relinquish, he couldn't, he loved her too much to lose her.

Airy took her seat on the plane and Seth sat beside her, she stood and asked the flight attendant for another seat.

Seth had taken all he could and realized he'd have her undivided attention and there would be no better time to attain her full attention. Grabbing Airy's hand he pulled her back down hard causing her to fall to her bottom on the chair, and turning toward the flight attendant he politely told her that the change in seating wouldn't be necessary. Glaring at Airy what he didn't say in words his dark eyes said loudly and she turned away from him. Nothing more was said until the flight was in motion.

Knowing that she wouldn't be impolite to the other passengers and raise her voice he grasped her hand within his so she couldn't pull away and declared, "I know you are upset and believed the lie I told before about touching the sphere, though I need you to listen to me and hear what I say." He lowered his voice even more leaned into her and said, "It was all a lie, I never touched the sphere I told them all of that to save you. So, you didn't have to touch it again, I couldn't lose you, Airy, I love you too much."

He was lying to her again and she couldn't understand why he would think she would fall for his deceit again. Was it amusing to him to cause her pain, did he have to keep stabbing her with his dagger? She was in tears, but she would not let him see her cry for her losses.

"Airy, I need you to know how I knew more than you did." She still wouldn't look at him though after a pause he barreled on speaking very softly, "I went through something similar to you. It took place at the little beach cabin almost immediately after we arrived. I began having extremely vivid dreams. The dreams showed me people who called themselves our ancestors, and they talked to me telling me things about their past here on our planet and showed me their life here and how they lived before they set out for a new planet to colonize. You see Airy I was chosen similarly to you. They came to me and I was afraid to tell you. At first, I couldn't believe what was happening, I thought it to be a dream, but it continued night after night, almost. First, I said nothing because I didn't want you to feel I was concocting it to make you feel better, or even take it to mean I was making fun of you, that I would pretend such a thing. They seemed to give me more information than you received, I didn't want you to doubt yourself or even feel excluded since they didn't contact you there. I was still trying to sort this out when we went to meet Zack. It was hard for me to believe but I had just begun when everything went down. Airy, I love you. I've loved you since the dinner at the hotel, I think. Can't you see I didn't want to hurt you or make you feel less for me also receiving information from the ancestors?"

Shifting in her seat Airy looked into Seth's eyes trying to see if she could distinguish if he was lying. His story seemed just as fantastic as hers and she remembered him doubting her. Did she have a right to believe this was all made up for her benefit? Why couldn't he also receive information? However, as she gazed into his large brown eyes, she noticed not only the pain that reflected outward but also a single tear that fell down his cheek. Smiling at him she asked, "Can you tell me more of what you know of them?"

A grin pierced his face and he said, "I'd rather tell you how much I love you and need you."

She smiled, "Yes, tell me that first."

. . ⚭ . .

WEEKS PASSED BY AS life slowly became normal again. Seth stayed with Airy and Dee while in Texas. His actual residence was Phoenix. They had both thought about what to do next, stay in Austin or move to Arizona when Dee suggested, "Airy, it's obvious you two can't keep your hands off each other why don't you do the logical thing and get married and start over together someplace that will make you both happy?"

"Dee!" Airy blushed.

"You know you are both thinking it, well at least the moving out part," Dee exclaimed.

Airy's face turned crimson, while steam, if it could be seen came from her ears as she turned toward her friend, "Well, thanks Dee for that awesome blurt, by the way, we need to leave for my parents' house they are waiting for us and it is a three-hour drive," Airy rambled then looked over at Seth who seemed just as embarrassed by Dee's poorly chosen words.

With quick goodbyes said, they were in the car driving for some time before Airy broke the silence and spoke, "Seth, I apologize for Dee's comment earlier. I didn't put her up to that I need you to know."

"I never thought you did." Her own need to apologize made him wonder if she wasn't interested in marriage. Well, he knew he'd find out soon because he planned to ask her at her parents. He'd thought about marrying Airy though was waiting for the right way to ask, not sure if a fancy restaurant was the right place or even the way Airy would like. He even wondered if getting down on one knee was something she'd like. However, he wished Dee hadn't put the thought in her head because he wanted her to be completely surprised.

· · ⚘ · ·

"SO, SETH, YOU HAVE been here for three days and I can tell you have something on your mind. I think I know but why don't you get it off your chest and tell me anyway?" John questioned the young man before him.

Whipping Seth out of his musing he looked at John Sheppard and said, "I have something important I want to ask your daughter though I can't seem to find the perfect way."

John looked at Seth and with years of experience, he made a statement hoping to give him insight. "It's been my belief that honesty and romance go hand in hand. A woman wants to see your affection reflected in your eyes when she looks at you. The surroundings are second to the love, my boy."

"But I want to give her it all, a beautiful proposal in the most wonderful way. The kind she will always remember."

"And you will because you love her. My advice is to think about what makes her smile and I know it will come."

That last statement sparked something within Seth and he grinned, gave John a quick handshake-hug, and left him without another word.

The following evening Seth put on his sports coat gathered everything he needed and waited downstairs in the foyer of the Sheppard's two-story home until his intended began to slowly descend the staircase. She had chosen a blue tea-length dress with sheer short sleeves draping her shoulders and the same sheer material made a belt that wrapped around her small waist accenting the petti form beneath. She was a picture of beauty and his mouth watering as he watched her body glide over the steps. Everything was planned and he couldn't wait to ask her to be his bride. He was glad she hadn't questioned him when he told her he wanted to go out for dinner just the two of them and asked her to wear a pretty dress because the restaurant was equipped with a dance floor.

She smiled once at the bottom and inquired, "Do you like?" she did a little twirl.

"Very much." He kissed her cheek and said, "Shall we?"

They drove only a short distance to Hermann Park Japanese Gardens. She questioned the restaurant's location but Seth said patients we have plenty of time before our reservation. They began strolling through the wonder of the gardens, walking under crepe myrtles while azaleas adorned with twinkly white lights lined the path. They moved forward past the dogwoods and cherry trees with a gentle breeze tossing their hair as they walked down toward the water and a small bridge. Standing on the bridge was a guitar player who strung his fingers across the strings as a soft romantic melody floated through the air making the trees around them dance. As they began to walk over the bridge Seth pulled Airy to a stop and took both hands in his as he went down on one knee. Gazing upward into her green eyes he said, "My heart has been yours since the night we strolled through beautiful gardens much like these in Africa, and now as I kneel here before you, I want to ask you to be my partner, my wife, and my strength for the rest of our days. Airy Sheppard, will you marry me?"

Airy pulled Seth to his feet and with eyes beaming she said gleefully, "Yes! Yes, with my whole heart, I love you, Seth Lock."

He placed the ring he held in his hand on her finger then brought it to his lips and kissed it and then her lips that shimmered in the dusty evening light.

Chapter Thirteen

Soft music played forcing Seth to wake. How long had he been sleeping he wondered as his heavy eyelids struggled to open. He blinked several times before he could fully look around. Feeling weighted he maneuvered his body lifting it from the bed. His eyes focused on the blue-green water stretching out before him. Walking toward the sliding glass door he rubbed his head, the fog within blanketing him. Looking around he felt confused. Seth remembered hitting a guard and rushing toward Airy to save her. What the hell was he doing in a house on the beach? With both hands, he opened the sliding door that stuck and slid with much effort on the metal runner. With weighted feet, he walked out and onto the white sand, while the sound of the waves approaching the shore met his ears like a soft melody. The blue sky rose above the water, and the warm air coming off the ocean smacked his face and body. A soft hand grasped him, and he turned to see Airy's radiant face. He reached out to caress her cheek.

"What....What are we doing here?" his voice sounded hoarse to his ears.

"What do you mean, my Love?"

"We were just in the lab in Africa. How did we get here?"

"Lab in Africa?" She looked at him questioningly, "Are you feeling, okay?"

He scanned the area, "No I...."

"Mommy, Daddy, come and play? Wanta make sand castle."

Seth looked down at a blond-haired little girl of about two years old. She looked just like her mother, and he smiled and then looked at Airy who went down to the child's level to answer her. The child quickly tootled off toward the house. "We have a... daughter?" he questioned aghast.

"Yes. What's wrong with you?"

"I don't remember anything after touching the sphere."

"What? I have to get you to a hospital."

"No. I feel a little lightheaded I need to sit. Did I hit my head?"

"No, not that you told me."

She directed him to a patio set so he could rest and she could keep an eye on Jordan while checking for any bumps or bruises. "Babe, are you saying you don't remember the last three years of our lives?"

"Yes, I think so. I remember being in Africa trying to save you from touching that sphere. There was a sphere?"

"Yes, my Love," she looked at him worriedly. "You and I both ended up converging on the sphere at the same time."

"What the hell happened, why can't I remember anything after?"

"Well, I can't speak to the latter but I can tell you about the sphere. Though shouldn't we get to a hospital first?"

"No. Please, tell me what happened."

"Okay, you remember throwing yourself at me and the sphere so that's where I will begin. When I touched it a shock of high electrical force went through me and somehow, I saw you coming at me, it was as if you were flying through the air. Everything went black and from what Dr. Chase told us we were unconscious for about two hours. We woke up in the infirmary and told him what we saw."

"What did we see?"

"We both described a kaleidoscope of lights and the object seemed to know the information it had already given so it gave us more comprehensive details. Do you remember?"

Seth thought for a moment and said, "Their skin was a greenish-blue color."

"Yes, anything else?" She could see him straining to think so she added, "It was a little closer to blueish than green to me but pale and pasty-like. They were tall maybe 12 feet, with large very dark eyes, and the head was much like a cone shape, while their arms went down past their hips, and their hands were portioned to their body size. They called the Earth Saysonie. They told us they could levitate and that is how they helped build the pyramids when they returned once, and they taught levitation to lots of the groups living on Earth, but the people somehow lost that ability. They traveled to the stars and other planets for more than a million years before they decided to leave the Earth. They said Mother Saysonie became increasingly violent, volcanos, seas, and the atmosphere were changing so fast after the continents started shifting more making it harder for them to breathe. The crops that used the old atmosphere were dying; however, they found other things to eat but they still couldn't make their bodies adjust to the transforming CO_2 levels. They tried to repair the earth but nothing helped. They could terraform the planet but it would take too long because first everything already existing would have to be eliminated and in doing so, the length it would take to renew would have killed them all off. With all their knowledge the only plan they had was to leave the earth."

"Yes, I remember. They built huge ships that could fly long distances and that is how they were able to get all the people into space. Before the last of them left they sent down pods like things that did terraform the earth in case they needed to return. A space station was set up at what we call Jupiter. That station was built hundreds of years before so it made sense to use it on their way to find more suitable environments. Not all things went easy even though they encompassed advanced technological abilities. It took thousands of years once in space and they even suffered major catastrophes events where they lost more than 100 thousand people in one accident. They said that many of their people were scattered as they searched and some were found later having made their homes in other solar systems and that living on the other planets changed them, some were unrecognizable when they met up later." He looked at her questioningly.

"Right," she answered.

Seth continued feeling good about his recall, "They said we are to tell this a little at a time so the people can adjust to it. They said they would fly ships in so they can be seen so we as a people will know this is true. They want to help us advance so we can leave the Earth because we are going to be hit by a comet in less than four hundred years. Of all the things they can do destroying a comet isn't one they can control. The impact will be fast and even more devasting than what happened when the asteroid hit and killed the dinosaurs.

They plan to help us advance in technology only in the areas needed but they said they cannot give us all they know quickly it would damage us, we are too underdeveloped to be able to grasp all, but they will teach us enough to help ourselves here and as we go forward into the stars. We have to begin preparing now developing ways to leave Earth. They have found a planet suitable for our people that they terraformed because the Kabyar's planet's atmosphere isn't appropriate for our lungs or bodies. They have been experimenting with us for years in order to see if we can survive on that terraformed planet. Changing our DNA to aid in our survival. Did I remember that correctly?"

"Yes, but I don't think we should let the world in on that one right away," she smiled.

"So, if I can remember that then why can't I remember the last three years?"

Airy was just as puzzled. It seemed weird that he remembered all of what they experienced with the device and yet he didn't know they married or had a child. "I think I should take you to the hospital Seth, I am worried that something is seriously wrong."

"Other than feeling foggy I feel fine."

Just then Jordan came up behind Seth and shouted, "Boo!" She laughed her childish laugh and asked, "Did I scare you?"

"Yes, my little Minion you did," he smiled at his daughter.

"Seth, you remembered."

"What?"

"That has been your, pet name for Jordan ever since she could talk."

"Yes, I gave it to her because once she started, she never stopped and followed me around asking questions."

"Right, she's inquisitive like her father, at almost two in a half."

"No, like you." He looked out at the water considering everything and said, "We bought this house after we married."

"Correct!" she yelled overjoyed that he was remembering.

"Airy, there had to be something that prompted this."

"Let's go see a doctor, now."

"How are we to explain? I lost my memory three years after I touched an alien sphere. No, correction, our ancestor's communication device. But yet I remember most of what they told us and beginning to recall my life piece by piece. No one will believe us; they will put me in an asylum. Talking about the sphere does the world know of it?"

"Yes, and no. After a lot of diplomatic talks, all the nations decided that they would let the world know slowly that aliens are real. That they sent the sphere to let us know that one day we would meet them and they promised to help advance us. A lot was left out about why they made contact now and being our ancestors. The governments hope they can work all that in the future, portions at a time. For now, governments around the world are acknowledging that Unidentified Spaceships are real, contact has been established with the world governments and they are viewed as harmless but helpful and inquisitive."

．． ⚓ ．．

SETH COULD FEEL THE ocean breeze across his dark skin and could smell the warm scent of fish and sand as he lay in bed trying to wake from the long night. The door was open to allow the air to cool the small house. Two days passed and Seth felt like his memory returned fully. His mind flashed suddenly to what caused him to open his eyes two days prior. Quickly he realized it was them again. Shooting up from the bed he grabbed his denim pants and blue polo shirt that lay on a chair beside the bed and raced outside to find his family.

Airy and Jordan were sitting on the beach singing nursery rhymes as they built sand castles. The tide was low so they were able to make them in the wet sand adding just enough of the dry so they would be erect. Jordan happily fetched the dry sand with her little bucket.

Seth stopped mid-step and looked at his family. He felt lucky to be in their little home able to enjoy the two most precious things in his life, but their lives like others were about to change in ways he couldn't fathom.

Chapter Fourteen

"Seth, this could have waited for morning." Airy looked down at Jordan who was rubbing her sleepy little eyes. Soon after he told her what he remembered, and he was sure that it was the cause of his temporary memory loss, he demanded they leave to catch a flight to the United States and Washington DC.

"Airy if we don't tell the president in person then I am afraid it will not be taken seriously."

"But what if he won't see you?"

"I thought about that and sent a message to General Turner and told him it was very important that I talk to our president and that the ancestors gave me a message for him, he replied via text message and said he'd try."

"So, you have heard nothing since?"

"No, but I sent another saying we were leaving tonight for Washington."

"I understand the implications of this message you received, although I still feel it could have waited for morning."

"He'll need the information quickly so as to execute plans with the rest of the world's governments." Seth bent and picked up his daughter, he adjusted her on his hip, and looking at his Jordan he asked, "Are you ready to go on your first airplane ride my, Minion?"

Jordan smiled shaking her head up and down animated she inquired, "Mommy, where's Bunny?"

"He's in your bag." Airy knew that Jordan couldn't sleep without her favorite stuffed animal by her side.

Once they were directed to their seats and settled themselves the flight attendant announced that all cell phones and electronics were to be turned off before the flight began.

Seth looked at his phone still no call or text from Turner. He reluctantly pushed the button on the side and watched as the screen went black.

Airy and Jordan slept a lot of the flight but Seth couldn't relax. What he needed to tell the president was too important for their civilization and the future. He was directed to inform the leader with the most influence on the other governments; Seth knew no one better than the now President of the United States, Mitchell Hatcher.

Hatcher entered West Point at 17 after graduating, served in the Navy for four years, and secured a law degree at Stanford University a short time later. After that, he went to work as counsel for a consortium of companies. He was elected to the Senate just four years later. Served for five years and then began working for the government at the UN. His negotiation skills were superb and earned him the Nobel Peace Prize at the tender age of 48. He then started his political career and road to the White House. He proved his abilities everywhere he went and became the 49th president at age 54. He knew no other powerful figures that would be as adept as President Hatcher in bringing all the leaders to the table to hear something that would change the world for the second time in three short years.

. . ⚜ . .

DISEMBARKING THE 20-hour flight left all with jet lag. Seth turned his phone on after they touched down and multiple alerts dinged for thirty seconds. He looked quickly finding the ones from General Turner first. He began reading one after the other and saw that arrangements were handled; he was set to see the president tomorrow at 12:30 right before his lunch and after a video call with the secretary of state.

Seth rushed Airy and Jordan through the terminal to the shuttle that would take them to their hotel. They all needed a good meal and rest.

They arrived at the Hilton Hotel in less than fifteen minutes and once they checked in and cleaned up, they went to the in-house restaurant for a much-needed meal. Seth apprised Airy when he was to meet the president and what he would say.

"I still find it hard to believe they forced all of this on you and in doing so it made you lose a piece of time. At least it was temporary." She said the last hoping it would make him feel better that he was being used like a pawn in a chess game. Airy felt grateful he'd confided in her after the sphere about the dreams he was given by the ancestors, though, his dreams were more words and feelings with some pictures, while hers were more of a vision of the past with narration.

"Yes, this time. What of the next? They may use you in the future. What if it does more damage or puts one of us in a coma again? Airy, I know it is important to our existence here on earth but I don't like or want to be the go-between, and if they try to use you, I may want to kill them."

"Thank you, Darling, but I know you are not that sort of a man."

"A man can be driven to kill. You and Jordan are my life and if anyone harms either of you, I will murder them, even if they are our alien ancestors."

Airy smiled at her husband the look on his face made her feel and believe he meant every word. It felt good to know he loved them that much and at the same time, she hoped it would never come to that. However, ever since he told her that he'd been abducted and taken into their ship and they put what he described as some sort of electrodes on his skull giving him more information and telling him exactly what to communicate, she felt that their lives were no longer their own. They were without choice; the ancestors could take them and make them do whatever they wanted. Extensively they were the ancestor's puppets and there wasn't a damn thing they could do to stop them from abducting them.

Seth pushed the food around on his plate. His stomach said he was hungry however, his thoughts were occupied with the assignment ahead of him; to tell President Hatcher that a fleet of ships was on their way, and in three short weeks he was to put together a meeting with all the heads of each country in one place. It had to be every leader. He is to obtain their agreement to come so the ancestors can speak to them at once, however, the kicker is that absolutely no security or weapons are to be in this one room where they were all to gather. He thought about the rest of the information and he wasn't certain if the president would even agree.

.. ⚜ ..

THE ALARM ON HIS PHONE went off and Seth pushed himself out of bed. The Hilton possessed some of the best accommodations. Late last night they all went for a walk hoping to relax, but unfortunately, it did little to take their minds off the situation. The nearby park was full of wonder for Jordan, she picked up leaves from the ground below the trees marveling at the different array. She liked how large and colorful they were, after spending most of her young existence on the beach the leaves were new to her.

Airy climbed out the other side of the bed gathering her clothes and said, "Keep an eye on Jordan and after we both finish our showers, we can go get some breakfast before you have to leave."

"Sounds like a plan, Darling," he stood and walked to Airy kissing her passionately. He realized that he'd been so preoccupied lately that they hadn't made love in days.

"Mmmm, that was nice, I've missed you."

"Me too." He took possession of her lips again and caressed her face before he said, "Off with you woman before we miss breakfast."

Airy giggled, "I didn't start this you came to me remember?"

"Yes, I know," he swatted at her bottom as she went to walk away.

· · ⚜ · ·

THE TIME WAS NEARLY noon as the shuttle to the White House dropped him off. Seth made his way to the door and just inside were guards and areas for people to go through metal detectors before they were allowed farther inside. Then there was a man with a tablet in his hands at a podium and he was directed there. The man behind the podium asked his name and who he was there to see. He pushed buttons on the tablet and then directed him to the second set of metal detectors and said, "Once you are cleared, go to the room on the right labeled waiting area 1, someone will come to get you when he is ready. Have a nice day."

Seth thanked him and did as directed. Once he was in the waiting area, he felt more nervous than before, he'd never met any president much less have a meeting with one. He replayed over and over what he would say and wished he'd constructed some notes ahead of time. But there was no need because the ancestors embedded the information in his brain.

Seth looked at his Apple smartwatch for the fifth time, 12:55 and he was still waiting, he sat alone in the waiting area. He prayed the president didn't forget he was waiting. Seth stood and started to pace the room, reading signs on the walls to pass the time. He glanced at his watch again 1:05 the door swung open startling him.

"Mr. Lock?"

"Yes," he answered anxiously.

"The President apologies for your wait, his schedule isn't always accurate though he is ready to see you now. This way please."

Seth's anxiety skyrocketed; he was about to talk to the President of the United States in person. He followed the young man down two corridors to an elevator, they proceeded to the second floor and the northwest corner to a room labeled President's Dining Room.

"The President said he had lunch prepared for you both since he was detained. I will introduce you and leave. I will be here in the hall when you are ready to leave to see you downstairs." They went inside and toward the back of the room were two men in black suits standing at the ready should anyone threaten the president.

President Hatcher looked up when the young man made the introduction and the President stated, "Nice to see you didn't give up on me, sorry for the delay."

"I am very sorry for interrupting your lunch."

"Nonsense, my other meetings went long. I hope you like Hoagies, when I am in a hurry, they are my favorite go-to." He leaned in close and said, "Plus they won't let me have them very often so I sometimes just say I am running late and need something light so they will make them for me," he laughed. "So, tell me about the ancestors, and then tell me what they want. I was told you are one of the only two people who have communicated with them successfully."

The man seemed like anyone else and put Seth at ease. "Yes, Sir. I am sure you have been briefed, so I will give you the highlights." He pulled out his chair and sat down. "They said the planet is doomed, but we as a people can do as they did and leave and go to the stars. They say that they have terraformed a planet not too far from here however it isn't perfect," Seth took a breath.

"Yes, they are ready to reveal themselves fully now to all. I suppose all the spaceships seen by the general public over the past three years weren't enough publicity. I am glad we informed the public last year that they were no threat. It fixed most of the panic that had begun," Hatcher stated.

Seth nodded as he took a bite of his sandwich and washed it down with a sip from the bottled Coke sitting in front of him. "Yes, Sir. They want a leader who can take charge to help them negotiate. The first thing they want is to meet with all the leaders from every country, they know everything about us and understand that they all have to agree, and they want no guards and no one extra in the room."

The president nodded and Seth continued when he'd said almost everything the president put down the last bit of his Hoagie, considering it for a few seconds, and responded, "Just how am I to get them all to agree to this?"

"I don't know, Sir. I know you are one of the best negotiators on our planet so I just hope you can pull a rabbit out of your hat for this one."

"Ok, however, I do know when someone is holding back and I can see it in your eyes so what's the rest."

Seth cleared his throat and began with, "President Hatcher, they expect all the cultures on this planet to give them ten people from each of our diverse cultures, five men and five women. They want to do testing on them to make sure we can survive on that new planet. After they are done with the testing, they want to take them to this new planet and leave them there to begin a new life. That is if the testing proves to them that they will be able to survive. They stressed that the people must be from each of the cultures, and they would like each of these people to be from 18 to 40 of our human years. They want a genetically perfect as possible match to their culture. Now I did a quick calculation on this and I know there are more than 3800, diverse cultures that number could be slightly higher. Then they want 10 people from each that would be an estimated 38 thousand people."

"What you are telling me is they want to seed this planet they have terraformed now, not later when we build the ships. Which by the way is going to be hard to convince the leaders if they can't see the destruction coming. Put that aside and tell people that only ten people from each ethnicity are to go, and I am certain from what you are saying that LGBQ is not allowed to be part, that these humans are to be of reproducing age and the rest of us have to stay in hopes these aliens are telling us the truth that they are going to help give us the technology, so what, are future great-great-grandchildren can leave Earth."

"Yes, Sir. The building of transportation to the new planet is going to take more than 100 years and then we gather all the population to leave. They want the world to have no more than one child per family so the population will be reduced. In seventy years, they will be on our planet full time teaching young people of 25 and less how to grow food that will sustain us on the journey, their technology, and astronomy among other teachings. They want to start that early so the next generation will already know this information."

"They want to talk to the leaders and explain it all."

Seth nodded.

Chapter Fifteen

The Circle Convention Center in Zurich Switzerland was chosen for the conference. Attached to an airport for convenience, however, what Hatcher liked best was that the large adjacent hotel could be bought out for the week. He scheduled everything to alleviate any pressure on the leaders so it wouldn't be an inconvenience. Arrangements were made to make their stay feel like a vacation therefore putting them at ease. All flights were postponed except the leaders coming into Zurich for the week.

The day was finally here and each country representative large and small was in one tremendous hall. Convention Hall B was selected; Hatcher chose small tables big enough for five leaders each which lent to a conversation so no one felt isolated. He made the staff place only people who spoke the same language together and he even insisted his staff verify each leader was not with another he or she didn't relate to or had a conflict with. That was the hardest part. Memo pads with pens were placed on the tables for each delegate. Today it was all coming together and he hoped they all would have patience and tack for the proceedings.

Every leader confirmed they had a reservation before entering the conference room. President Hatcher received word all were in attendance and the event could begin. Nearing the appointed time Hatcher looked toward Seth and nodded his head and then took his place on a small stage in front of everyone. Thankful for the ancestor's device that allowed all languages interpreted so there was no need for additional personnel or anyone outside this room to know what took place.

"If everyone will please take your seats we will begin." Then stepping to the side, he spoke to Seth before again going to the podium. Clearing his throat to hush the room and draw attention to himself. Everyone in the room was anxious and fell silent since they knew that the aliens were coming today and for the first time, they would be able to look upon them. "We all know that today is very momentous for all of mankind. Before I introduce our guest, I would like to remind all that tomorrow we will continue any needed discussion on today's agenda. A briefing on the main topic was sent to you already and I urge you to write down any questions on the notepads provided so that we may ask questions. I want to thank each of you for participating in this global event. Now for our guests to be comfortable there are a few things we need to do." He nodded toward Seth who was now at the doors in the front of the room. In seconds the room dimmed and a soft red light came on. There was plenty of white light just not as overpowering as before.

Seth walked over to the exit door on the east side and opened it. A black-cloaked hooded form appeared. Seth stood six feet and this cloaked figure's stature was a head shorter. All eyes in the room were on them as they made their way to the stage. The room was deathly silent. Seth stood back as the figure stepped on the platform and stood by President Hatcher. It looked at the president for a brief time and then turned toward the group made a small bow-like gesture and pushed the hood backward off of its head.

The room exploded, not with noise, but as if everyone was holding their breath in anticipation to see what it looked like beneath the cloak, so it was similar to air being expelled by everyone at once.

The short grayish alien's head was round without hair, and his large inset dark black bottomless eyes stared at the people. Its fingers were only four and they were long and spindly things with no obvious nails only pointy tips.

In the minds of everyone, at once, the alien spoke, "Do not fear me, my name is Tooish and I look different from you because of my time in space and the planet we came to call our home."

The congregation of leaders looked at one another all wondering if their neighbor heard what they did. They were told this was how they communicated though it was still unexpected.

Again, the character spoke to everyone at once, "We sent a message that every leader be told of our existence and since everyone is here, I know from reading your thoughts this is true. I desire to tell you everything you want to know though first I ask you allow me to inform you what is to come and how we plan to help your kind." The alien proceeded to tell the group of the impending comet. The destruction that would proceed on planet Earth and how they wanted to help all mankind survive. With the plan laid out, he added that they were going to need people from all ethnic groups to participate in testing to make sure that all could survive once they arrived on the new planet. He stated the timetable and how humans would begin cultivating new foods that would sustain them on the great ships, and once they arrived at the new planet. He told them all of the new metal that would be used to build and that some new technology would be granted for building purposes.

All this took a toll on the ancestor and nearly two hours later he informed everyone that he needed to go back to his ship to recover and that he was only able to stay for a short time in this atmosphere without an apparatus on. He requested that all go and return at 6 p.m. for him to answer any questions they may have. With that, he turned and placed the hood on, and began to walk to the east door that he came in. A beam of light transported him to the waiting spacecraft.

When the celestial form exited the room everyone within jumped from their seat and loud conversations activated in the room. Hatcher was speaking with Seth but was interrupted by Russia's leader along with Ukraine's questioning him on what Tooish meant when he said experiments on people.

Hatcher excused himself and went directly to the podium. "Please everyone understand that I know no more than you do at this time. Tooish will return and we will be able to ask our questions of him. At the front exit, there is a box that has tickets inside with numbers on them you will be able to draw a ticket yourself and the number on it will be yours and in sequence, the first question will be asked. Write down many inquiries in case someone else solicits yours to Tooish. You will be allowed to ask only one question.

Please go eat and make sure you return on time. Please this is crucial no speaking about anything you heard in this room with anyone, save all communication for now within these walls. Thank you all for your patience." With that President Hatcher turned and walked out of the room.

. . ⋈ . .

THE DOOR TO ROOM 3028 opened and Seth stepped inside, Airy waited patiently at the chair by the patio window. Seth grabbed a bottle of water from the mini fridge and sat down next to his wife. He'd never had such an exhausting day for having done nothing but listen.

"You look worried, my Love?" Airy looked at her husband tenderly.

"I am, I have a strange feeling and I haven't been able to shake all day."

"Do you care to tell me about it?"

"I would if I could, I can't explain it. Let's relax on the bed together I would like nothing more than to make love to my wife."

Airy stood and moved to Seth, she knelt in front of him and began to run her hands up and down his thighs. "How long do we have?"

"About three hours, I think we can accomplish that in time for me to return to the conference." Leaning forward Seth placed his hands lovingly on each side of Airy's face before his mouth descended on her plump red lips. They were warm and inviting like he knew they would be and it calmed him to just touch her. It always seemed like the first time each time he made love to her and he needed her more now than he'd ever needed her before. Needed to feel her warm supple body against his, needed her tenderness, her love, but more than that he needed her strength.

They stood and quickly undressed each other. After all their clothing was discarded, they stood naked, their bodies naturally molding together. A stream of feverish kisses took flight between them until at last they needed to join and found their way to the bed. He took her quickly to the brink of ecstasy and then suddenly stopped. Leaping from the bed as if something plucked him from her arms, he stood dazed for a moment as Airy looked on with concern.

"Seth, what's wrong?"

He stood shaking his head. She rose swiftly from the bed and went to his side, "Seth what is going on? What is it? Tell me please?" her concern was evident.

Taking her hands in his he moved to the bed where they both seated themselves. He looked into her eyes, "Airy, I just had a flashback." He shook his head unsure of what it meant. "I want to tell you a story of something that took place in my teen years. Randy Manning was my best friend and he was moving away from Michigan, Bay City. I told you I grew up there. We were fifteen at the time, anyway, he was leaving the following weekend so we took the opportunity to go to the lake one last time, Saginaw Bay. We were in the water for probably an hour and darkness came upon us so we spent the remaining time on the beach. I pulled a couple of beers from my backpack, which I stole from the refrigerator before I left the house. You know to have a good send-off, anyway, I remember we both saw a light in the distance. We walked toward it and it flashed several colors and then we were lying on the ground by the rocks. We both thought it weird but it was late and we didn't want to get into trouble so we got on our bikes and raced home. The following day Randy wouldn't talk to me when I called. I phoned several more times and his parents said he requested that I stop calling. I went to see him and again he wouldn't see me, then they moved. I have always wondered why and I just figured it out when my eyes were shut, when that memory appeared. It was as if a light turned on in my brain and I remembered everything. No, probably not everything but enough to make some things clear. I saw the flashing lights and it was….a flying saucer."

"All this time you didn't remember?"

"No. I recall a few crazy dreams after that night but I didn't remember anything until now about the spacecraft. Randy must have remembered and he freaked out about it, so much so he didn't want to even see me."

"Are you saying you have been visited before that tiny shack we stayed after I was in a coma and before our house at the beach in Australia?"

"Yes. They took us both up into their ship I remember Randy screaming when I flashed back a few minutes ago. I don't recall anything else about the ship, but I do remember a few of my dreams shortly afterward, even after all this time. They weren't something you forget. Aliens from another world were doing experiments on my body, they looked just like Tooish short and big insect with black eyes. I remember an incision on me that I couldn't account for after one of my dreams and it was where they were twisting some sort of metal device into me. I believed it to be a nightmare. I was a teenage boy, I figured I cut myself on something though it was something that was done to me. I never thought about the incident being real not a dream. I recall the sore taking a long time to heal. It was them, the ancestors, they did that to me causing terrible pain. How can I believe they won't harm us today?"

"Did you say short and large insect eye?"

"Yes."

"When we touched the stone and the ancestors communicated with me, with you, they were tall blueish green and their eyes were a bit larger than ours but they fit their frame. Babe, something is terribly wrong."

"You're not thinking that these aliens are not our..."

They both spoke at the same time, "Not our Ancestors."

"That can't be. No, there is a reasonable explanation. Probably just their prolonged stay in space changed them from what their bodies were when they were on the earth versus outer space. I was young and maybe I am mixing things up." Seth said trying his hardest to reason out their change, and what happened to him and his friend.

"I assume that could account for it. Was there anything else that seemed different from what you remember in your dream when you were young and your experiences with them now?"

He considered her question and then replied, "No they seem the same. Though when I look at Tooish I feel an uneasiness."

"Okay, I think we should each make a list of things and feelings we remember from our interactions or dreams and see how that plays out. We shouldn't jump to the wrong conclusion because a few things aren't matching."

"Good idea."

It was late, nearing the six o'clock meeting time. Seth glanced over his sheet and handed it to Airy. "I need to get downstairs to the convention hall check our lists and see if you find any major discrepancies."

She looked at his and then at hers again and nothing stood out. Descriptions of the knowledge that was imparted were for the most part mirrored. The only difference seemed to be looks. "Seth, is there any way to get me into that hall I'd like to see him and maybe talk to him myself."

"No, sorry, Babe. That is by their request, only leaders and of course me."

"Since I received their communication first, you would think I'd be allowed."

"I'm not certain they know you received information since it was delivered on that sphere and not more personal as mine."

"So, they have never conversed about my involvement?"

"No, I assume since they did so with me, they didn't feel the need to bring you into this." He straightened his tie in front of the mirror by the door, and asked, "Do I look okay?"

Airy glanced at her husband and then went over to him centered his tie on his dark burgundy shirt and said, "That's better. I love you."

Seth bent down and placed a quick kiss on her lips, "I love you too. It's late, see you soon as this wraps up." He turned and opened the door departing.

Airy sat down in the chair again and picked up the papers. She read through them again and the same result was obtained. She stood went to the sliding door and moved onto the small balcony. Looking out over the land she thought about her visions though something caught her eyes. She blinked several times taking in the image before her. The silver circler ship hovered over the airport area closest to the hotel. A beam of light shot down from its center to the ground. Two cloaked figures emerged from the beam seaming to float towards the hotel. One removed his hood as they moved together. Airy's breath caught in her throat. Stunned she raced out of the room not even bothering to put her shoes on. She ran to the elevator pushed the button for the ground floor and prayed she'd get to Seth before they shut the convention room doors.

The elevator opened to the ground floor and she shot out pushing her way through a crowd of people just outside. She caught sight of the cloaked forms down a long corridor that led outside the building. Then she couldn't move. It was as if she were frozen in place. She tried to talk, then yell, but nothing exited her mouth. Even the people around her seem to be immobilized. In horror, she watched as the two cloaked aliens made their way into the side entrance of the large convention hall. When at last the doors closed her body gained mobility and she stumbled as her forward motion began. With a splat, she fell to the floor.

Her mind felt jumbled; a voice poured in making the fog lift as it said, "You will not interfere, your mate's life is at stake, go back to your room and all will be forgiven." Airy felt a chill run up her spine. Pushing herself with all her strength she managed to stand and tried again to go toward the hall where the delegates were assembling, she fell back to the ground paralyzed. It felt like minutes ticked by as she sat motionless on the carpeted floor, the people around her didn't move either it was as if the world had suddenly stopped. They were powerful, more so than she imagined. Closing her eyes for several seconds and gathering her thoughts, her energy, and her nerve; mustering everything within her she struggled to stand once more, and the room began to revolve again. She strained to go toward the conference room but her legs wouldn't budge but instead seemed to turn her body toward the elevators.

Chapter Sixteen

Airy anxiously awaited her husband's return. Should she tell him any of what she experienced? If she did, would he be in danger like she was told, would she for that matter? Never in her wildest dreams would she expect her life to change so radically because of an excavation. That was the point where her life went haywire. The only good things out of it were Seth and Jordan, but she could lose them if she told Seth or anyone. No, she was on her own and she must fight to find a way to handle these powerful beings so her family as well as the world was safe.

• • ⁕ • •

THE CONFERENCE WAS a month ago and the aliens had begun bringing materials for the building of the first ship. Seth's own fears over the ancestors and his first encounter were pushed down. Airy hated not saying anything about what happened, to Seth but she knew it was for the best, though she gave him subtle hints making him question the ancestors. She couldn't help herself. She wasn't technically informing him just playing on his anxiety hoping that he would recognize the deception on his own. The only thing she knew at this junction was that she must go to the beginning to figure out what she suspected was true.

• • ⁕ • •

"AIRY, I CAN'T LEAVE now."

"I understand but I must. When a friend asks for your help, you go if you can, right? I promise only to be gone as long as I need to."

"What about Jordan?"

"Since we stayed for a while with your parents, I thought she could stay in Texas with mine. I spoke to Mom and they are looking forward to having her with them for a week or more."

"So, you have already taken care of everything, I feel like I am the last to know."

"Seth, I just wanted to sort out all the details before I told you. There was no need to add to the many things you already are dealing with. Angela is going through a bad breakup and I will only be gone a short while."

"All the way to England to comfort a friend? A friend you never mentioned in the almost four years that I have known you."

"I told you we were in high school together and later in college. Sweetheart, you have been very busy helping out the efforts to make the world unified on all the alien's wants, and I have just been sitting here each day. I need something to occupy my time. I didn't think staying with a friend for a week or more to help her through this traumatic time would be an issue for us. I will call her and cancel if that is what you wish." Airy had no intentions of doing so it was a ploy she was sure would work, and it did.

"No, you are right she needs a friend and you could use a distraction. I will just need to let work know I won't be there, so I can take you to the airport, after all, they are giving me a paycheck." Seth also realized that it was the perfect time for Airy and their daughter to be away. He only hoped he would be able to sort things out without getting himself killed.

"That will be great, Babe." She hated lying to him though there wasn't another way. She was just glad his uncle Stephen got the information she needed and said he would keep her secret to himself, though he didn't understand why.

. . ⚜ . .

AIRY'S CONNECTING FLIGHT took her to Leeds Bradford Airport which lay 21 miles from her destination RAF Menwith Hill military base which was run by the US and UK together. This base dealt with intelligence and communication and was the perfect place for the sphere to be sent for further analysis. When she arrived, she didn't exactly know what she expected but it wasn't this grand site. So many satellite arrays and too many structures to count.

When she disembarked her taxi at the gate, they gave her a name badge and an escort to take her to her destination. Professor Morard saw to it that the scientists who were conducting tests on the globe-shaped communication device were informed of her arrival and her ability to make it work.

Her escort was a young private most likely just out of high school. He was polite and only talked when needed. They walked in silence most of the way before he said, "The next building is where I am to take you. Once at the door he opened it and a guard inside looked at her badge and directed her inside shutting the private out as he did. He ran a metal-detecting device up and down her body before leading her down a long hallway. He used a keycard to open the door at the end and then directed her in.

Airy went inside the door frame and looked around. The room was substantial. A man rose from his desk as she entered and looking at her name tag uttered, "Your presence is requested by Dr. Standage who is in charge."

As Airy followed she pondered if they would allow her to do what she needed or if she would even gain access. An elderly man now stood before her and was introduced as Dr. Standage. She shook his hand, "Thank you for allowing me to intrude on your work."

"Nonsense this isn't an intrusion. Come let me show you some things we have accomplished and you can tell me about your experiences with the sphere."

He told her everything they accomplished and how they extracted information with a computer AI they hooked up to the sphere. Their research and what they found out was astonishing and now it didn't have to be touched to gain information. "Dr. can we ask it any questions?"

"You know we haven't tried. Once we plugged in the AI it just started feeding information and that was only a week ago, but for some reason, the computer shuts off after two hours. It is though it over-exhilarates the computer." He laughed then asked, "Did you have something in mind?"

"Yes, though it is confidential. A matter of security I hope you understand." She hated lying though this was the only way to protect everyone involved.

"I would think I hold a ranking in security matters."

"Not on this. President Hatcher sent me personally to take care of this. He wasn't certain I could get the information, however for the governments of the world, I was going to put my life on the line to try and get them some answers. Though now with your AI attachment, I may not have to risk my life."

"Whatever is needed. Let's go talk to the programmers and get them to start working on how to ask questions."

It was three more days before they said they formulated a program that would request information. All that is needed is someone to man a computer to type in the question and then the AI would in essence talk to the communication sphere. They tried it once by inquiring the name of the home planet they now live on and the answer came back as Sidko so they knew the answer was correct.

Airy was elated she would finally have her answers and she prayed that she was wrong. She sat down in front of the computer keyboard, then looked around and inquired, "I will need privacy for this please." They all looked at one another. Dr. Standage cleared his throat and shooed everyone away. Airy began to type and after a while, most of her queries were resolved and her fears were realized.

Booking a flight to her parents immediately after she returned to her hotel Airy wondered what she was supposed to do with the information she now possessed. The imposters said that Seth would be harmed if she interfered. But the world believed in what the aliens said they were here to do. As far as she knew they could be here to help though, it wasn't likely since they lied about their identity. The ancestors said they would be coming and yet, they were not here on Earth as far as she knew because why would they allow the imposters to claim themselves as the ancestors? Why were they not stopping them? Who were these extra-terrestrials and how did they know what the ancestors communicated to herself and Seth? She wished she'd thought of asking those questions while she was at the base. Then it occurred to her that the pretenders had read her mind at the conference in Switzerland and that meant that they read hers and Seth's before, most likely months before, corresponding with Seth's abduction out of their bed when he lost a part of his memory for a short time. That must mean they have been here on Earth for quite a while or at least in their proximity. So, if this scam were known to the governments and the people of the world how would they ever be able to trust the true ancestors in the future?

All of this Airy felt was best allocated to someone in power or at least someone proficient at solving problems and was able to enforce some way to correct this global mess. The challenge was who to trust and did she doom Seth and herself as well as that person and the world, since the entities were so powerful?

. . ⚕ . .

HOBBY AIRPORT IN HOUSTON was bustling with people as Airy picked up her bag from the conveyor belt. Her flight was on time and she knew her father would be punctual. Rounding the corner to walk toward the front door, she found her father waiting in the lobby.

They walked out to the covered parking areas as he talked about Jordan's remarkable talents. Observing his daughter's distraction, he knew she was upset and the only way to get her to open up was if they were alone. So, he suggested they stop at Barker's Bar-B-Que Shack not far from the airport. They made their way inside to a table in the back. Once they ordered John looked at his daughter and said, "Spill it, I know something has you in knots. When you left for England, it was evident and it seems now whatever it was has gotten worse. Don't tell me it's nothing."

"Dad, sometimes I wish you couldn't read me like you do, and yes there is something though I can't divulge it."

"Why not? You told us about everything that went down in Africa even when you were told to keep it to yourselves until the world was informed."

"Yes, that's true but we knew you would keep it a secret."

"And we did, so what's changed?"

Airy thought for a moment and wondered to herself, 'What has changed, she didn't think the aliens would be monitoring her in Texas. They weren't in England when she was there so she felt this far away must be safe.' "Dad, I will disclose although, I needed you not to breathe even a hint of this to anyone including Mom. Can you handle that?"

"If you think that is best, but I don't want to lie to her."

"You won't if you just say nothing. This is something that could damage the governments of the world as well as the people and maybe even get us killed." She looked around to make sure no one was seated near them. This little mom-and-pop barbeque shack didn't seem to have cameras. Moving in closer to her dad so she could see if anyone came near. "Dad, what I found out could affect everyone." She started with Switzerland and ended with the information she asked the orb in England.

John Sheppard considered everything his daughter expressed, "Is there any way to talk to the ancestors themselves? I think they would be the ones to set this right? After the power you say the imposters possess then we don't have a chance of succeeding."

"I know no way to physically get to the ancestors."

"Then to me, you have one recourse and that is the president. Airy, I know you are afraid for Seth; however, he has the right to know what is happening too."

"If I tell him they could read his mind, they might read mine again. No, Dad, I absolutely won't put him in further danger."

"How will you get to the president to warn him, that is if he believes you? After all, it was Seth who originally brought the imposters to him. He may choose to believe in them because at this junction your husband will back up what they say because he knows no difference."

"I know you are right but I must try. I hope you and Mom will keep Jordan here where she is safe until this can be resolved."

"Whatever you need, baby," he'd called her 'baby' all her life. It was his special nickname for her.

"Right now, I just need to hug my child and then my husband."

"Hey, what are your mother and myself chopped liver?" he laughed trying to break the tension he knew she felt.

"I already gave you a hug but I think I have a spare for Mom," she smiled knowing he was trying to help relax her before she made it home, so she wouldn't let her anxiety upset the family.

. . ⚜ . .

AIRY AWOKE TO A BRIGHT light filtering through the window. Jordan was lying on the bed asleep beside her. Something was outside and for some reason, she knew there was nothing to fear. Airy stood slipped a pair of jeans on and tucked in her nightgown as she walked toward the window. A group of glowing beings stood by the big oak tree in the backyard. They waved for her to come to them. She felt her body move and realized she was floating above the floor toward the bedroom door, and then through the kitchen, out the backdoor. There was no distress, she felt surprisingly light and a euphoria of sorts. Her body glided as she approached the forms.

In her mind, she heard, "You are Airy the woman that our sphere communicated with two days ago and again three years back are we correct?"

"Yes, but how did you know to find me here?"

"You were imprinted on the sphere and it gathered everything about you. From that, it wasn't difficult to find you."

"Have you come to help?"

"We have come to give you something that will aid in your quest to make the Alkean race expose themselves." They handed Airy a silver oval-shaped gadget that showed a white light on top and explained that when it started to blink, she was to press on the light.

"What will it do?"

"It will cause them to tell the truth to anything you ask as long as you don't stand more than ten feet from them. Do not let them see it, and clear your mind of all but questions or they will harm you. Airy we thank you for realizing they are pretenders. We became aware of the situation but until you communicated with our sphere, we were unsure how to correct this. We arrived shortly after them and have been attempting to find out all they have done."

"Why can't you handle them yourselves?"

"If we do your people will have reason to distrust. It must be you. Do not fear we will be nearby monitoring you."

Airy woke up and found herself in her bed with the oval object in the pocket of her jeans. It wasn't a dream though she felt like she'd been given a key without a lock.

· · ⚜ · ·

TWO DAYS PRIOR PRESIDENT Hatcher listened to Airy explain everything she knew with General Turner by her side. With a plan agreed upon to expose Tooish they waited for the arranged day.

Airy knew going into this meeting today that Seth would be there and she wished it was possible to share with him what transpired but there were already too many at present that knew to suspect danger, and though precautions were taken didn't mean it would go as arranged.

With the metal object in her hand, in her dress pocket, Airy walked with the president to the huge airplane hangar bay where they were storing all the materials that were given to them to start work on the ships for their so-called upcoming voyage.

• • ⚜ • •

TOOISH DRIFTED INTO the bay, and for a split-second, Seth wondered if he was doing the right thing and if he would even survive in the end. Committing himself he questioned Tooish, "You have told me there are only a few more items before you will set out the blueprints to build, but I must question why if we are to build a spacecraft, we have yet to receive the necessary components and needed materials?"

"As you said there are more items to come."

"You have been deceiving us," he fumed. "I know from experts that we will need countless more materials as well as electronics to build anything the scope needed to travel with thousands or even millions to outer space."

"I see you no longer trust and have brought in others to question this project. Now I can no longer use you."

Seth suddenly felt paralyzed. He was standing but incapable of moving or speaking.

Suddenly the doors to the bay flew open. Tooish turned to see President Hatcher, a young woman he recognized, along with Hatcher's

Secret Service personnel enter. He positioned himself in front of Mr. Lock and began to float toward them.

"Tooish it is good to see you I and Mrs. Lock have come to see the progress of her husband and yourself."

The group stopped feet away from Seth, and Airy wondered why her husband didn't join their party but she needed to concentrate on the mission at hand while not giving away their intent. Pointing the object within her pocket at Tooish and pushing the light she demanded, "Tooish, tell me are you, our ancestor? What race are you?"

He quickly answered, "I am Alkean." His face appeared to twist sideways with anger and he took a few steps backward.

Airy moved forward with the Secret Service and continued, "Why are you here imposter?"

He answered, "To take minerals from this planet and make the humans our slaves."

The President shook his head and several guards rushed forward. Tooish made a move away from Hatcher and Airy back toward Seth. He reached out grabbed Seth around the neck and said, "I will kill him. Do not come near me."

"Tooish, you lied to all the world and you think you can get away with this? My men will kill you if you do not let Mr. Lock go," the president demanded.

"No, they will not, and for that matter, I will get you all to do what I want." He gazed at Airy, his eye brightening, "I told you not to interfere." He began to move with Seth in front of him.

"Let him go," she demanded distracting him.

One of the Secret Service agents grabbed Seth and pulled him away from Tooish while another amid his gun, but Tooish suddenly disappeared.

President Hatcher motioned to his agent who looked down toward his breast as he spoke. "Search for Tooish or any aliens outside now." Nodding toward the other agent he left to join the search.

Airy was on the floor beside her husband who had crumpled to the floor as Tooish fled.

Seth looked at her, "I knew you were up to something when I spoke to Uncle Stephen however; I had no idea you were about to take on an alien."

Stephen stepped out from behind some boxes with a gun in his hand and as Airy helped her husband to stand she felt the hard metal object tucked in the back waistband of his trousers. The agent guarding the president jumped in front of him with his weapon still drawn now pointing it at Stephen who quickly dropped the gun and put his hands up.

Seth swiftly shouted, "Don't shoot he's with me. I also suspected Tooish of deception and placed Professor Morard, my uncle, there for protection in case something unsuitable happened. And it did. Just what the hell are you doing here Airy with the president and how did you get Tooish to confess?"

"You once said I was a strong capable woman, well I never knew how strong I needed to be to make sure he was exposed." Airy turned toward Hatcher, "Mr. President thank you for believing in me."

"With General Turner backing you and some inconsistencies on the material content that Seth created for me, I had already established a military committee to look into my suspicions."

"But Airy, how did you get him to just confess?"

"The real ancestors helped me reveal their plan with this." She took the metal object out of her pocket and showed him, then said, "This device makes them tell the truth. I suspected them at the summit and needed to confirm. They were too powerful for me to expose until the ancestors helped. I was unable to communicate their deviousness until now because lives were threatened."

"In the plane, I told you to create your own results, I think you finally achieved them. I just didn't realize it would be detective work."

"At the time I didn't realize it would be you and Jordan and our life together."

• • ⚜ • •

AIRY WAS GLAD THE IMPOSTERS were uncovered and the real ancestors were to arrive in two days to meet with the president. Her family was together again, and as she lay in bed next to her husband, wrapped in the safety of his arms, she wondered if it was truly over.

Seth seemed to read her thoughts and said, "I am curious about the Alkean and feel we haven't heard the last of them."

"I was pondering the same thing. They didn't put up much of a fight and then vanished."

"Airy, next time I want you to trust that I will take care of all of us, and not go rogue."

"I promise I will try."

"He turned her face toward him and said, "You don't sound convincing."

"Well, how do I convince you."

A mischievous grin took over his features and he pulled her to him. Airy giggled like a schoolgirl as his lips took possession of hers. They kissed one another like it was the first time their lips touched. Taking the other's soul as their warm hands caressed the other's body. Airy felt the carnal tingle develop within her womb, and sensed it flow along every nerve. His hand moved along her shoulder tugging her tank top strap downward as her hands pulled the bottom of his favorite blue t-shirt up until his torso was free. She laid a line of kisses from his lips to his neck and down his chest full of curly brown hair.

Seth pushed his wife back on the bed helping her to strip off the barrier between them. When they were both finally free, he took her on a leisurely ride to the brink of ecstasy. Kissing her temple then trailing a surplus of passionate kisses down her face stopping at her green eyes that fluttered shut, then to her small nose and cheeks before they paid homage to her lips again. She thrashed around begging him to give her the release of pleasure they both craved taking them to the statuary of closeness that bonds two souls together in passion, in love, forever.

Milton Keynes UK
Ingram Content Group UK Ltd.
UKHW020631070524
442340UK00006B/301